CIRCLE OF SIN

Also by March Hastings

Abnormal Wife
Again and Again
The Boys of Brigham Dee
By Flesh Alone
Crack-Up
The Demands of the Flesh
Design for Debauchery
Enraptured
Fear of Incest
The Heat of the Day
Her Private Hell
The Jealous and Free
Obsessed
The Outcasts
A Rage Within
Savage Surrender
The Soft Way
Three Women
The Third Sex
The Third Theme
The Unashamed
Veil of Torment
Whip of Desire

CIRCLE OF SIN

MARCH HASTINGS

ISBN-13: 978-1-954840-27-0

Published by
Cutting Edge Books
PO Box 8212
Calabasas, CA 91372
www.cuttingedgebooks.com

CHAPTER ONE

THE WISE GUY banged his whiskey glass on the table and yelled up to her. "Come on, Sarine, take it off!"

She leaned back against the pillar, and her slow laugh rolled over the audience. She winked to the piano player and he started the opening chords of her song, playing in his slightly off-beat rhythm. She began to hum low in her throat.

The men waited at their tables, quiet and tense. They sensed something different about Sarine tonight. Her voice, her smile, her whole being leaned closer to them. They didn't notice the watered-down drinks, they didn't care how much Cozy gypped them as long as Sarine held her sun-bronzed body within reach. An extended hand could almost touch the triangle of thigh that showed through the slit of her gown.

Sarine began to sing in her throaty, lazy voice.

As she worked over the melody, she counted the empty tables. Not bad for a Thursday. But she would have to give them something special tonight, some kind of powerful bait that would jam them back in tomorrow. She'd made up her mind that every two-bit sucker in this two-bit town would be fighting for a table when Jerry Lutha came to catch her act. Now, after six months of maneuvering, she had it all lined up. Tomorrow at midnight, Jerry Lutha would be listening to her voice.

She watched Cozy tugging at the points of his vest. He stood at the bar looking fat and dapper and anxious to get her home with him tonight. Sarine crooned in his direction, enjoying the way he nodded and smiled in return. She didn't give a damn about Cozy. What he had done for and to her was all in the game of getting to New York some day. She had sung around and slept around and Cozy was just another guy along the road to a big-time contract.

As Paul wound up the number, Sarine ambled over to the piano.

"Give me a strip beat," she said just loudly enough for him to hear.

He looked up from the keys with that questioning expression that always made Sarine nervous.

"Let's go, boy," she said. If only there were some way of shaking some life into him, that man could be a terrific success. Pity for so much talent to be wasted on someone who had no fight. She would have to drag him to New York with her.

Paul started a hip-swinging tune and she strode back on the stage.

The wise guy started clapping in time to the music and in a moment others eagerly joined him. Sarine began to rock her body with shrewd calculation. The whiskey, the smoke-laden air, the everyday boredom fueled her audience with vicious energy.

"Take it off!" the wise guy yelled.

"Let's see those legs, Sarine."

"Go, girl, go!"

She raised her arms high in the arc of spotlight and sent a quivering motion down the length of her body. Even with her eyes closed Sarine could see her audience. She could feel her control over them. Her body was like a whip and she used it to beat these men into desire. Even Cozy would be sweating beneath his starched shirt.

Only the cool notes of Paul's piano were aloof. Sarine tilted her head in the direction of the piano player and smiled at him. He too was watching her, but only to make sure that he kept the proper tempo for her dancing. His lean body bent over the keys as the long fingers stroked out the melody.

Purposely she slurred the words of her song, teasing them off her tongue and winding them around the room as if to capture the perspiring bodies and turn them in toward her.

Now they all leaned forward. She saw the hope in their greedy eyes. Their expectation licked at her and she laughed back, knowing how they loved to be made fools. She let her fingers stray over her body, slowly, tempting their thoughts. She touched her breast, and it was as though she felt each man touching it through her own fingers. When she slid her palm along her ribs, she saw their lips half open with tense dreams of fulfillment.

They were all hers. Every man in this room she could have at whatever price she might name.

She stood with legs spread wide apart, pulling the material of her dress tight across her belly and stretching her fingers stiffly out toward the darkness. Even the wise guy could say nothing now. He sat sprawled out in his chair, swallowing and watching.

He would come back tomorrow night. And so would they all, she knew. Because not one man of them would sleep tonight without dreaming of Sarine's vibrant flesh.

She took a quick bow and left the platform, listening to the wild applause that clamored for her body.

In her dressing room, she flicked on the fan and stood before its cooling breeze. The coolness swept over her skin as she slid out of her dress. Someday she would have an air conditioner and a room large enough to park a car in instead of this makeshift hole.

The sound of Cozy's footsteps interrupted her thoughts with irritation. She was in no mood for his nonsense tonight.

He burst into the room without bothering to knock.

"What was all that?" He ran worried fingers through his hair, ruffling the kinky curls into wild corkscrews. "What kind of cheap show do you think you're putting on here?"

"Oh, quiet down."

She took a bottle of witch hazel and patted some along her calves. Tomorrow, if the weather held, it would be a good idea to get out on the beach for one final, even tan before Jerry Lutha saw her.

"Don't you tell me to quiet down. Think I'm running a sex house all of a sudden?"

Sarine handed him the bottle of witch hazel and turned her back for him to massage.

Instinctively he obeyed, slapping the liquid against her shoulder blades and massaging it into the muscles of her neck.

"Well, answer me," he said. "I only own this place, you know."

How long had she been putting up with him? Six months, but it felt like forever. It wasn't the noise itself that she minded so much, but the fact that the noise never amounted to anything. That one person could yell so much and do so little often made her wonder how he came to be owner of the Jingo Club.

"You may own this place," she said, ignoring his fingers massaging her where they didn't have to, "but you don't own me."

She could have said a lot more but it was after three o'clock and there was no sense in arguing all night. A slight headache had begun to knot the muscles in her neck. If she could only get to sleep tonight—alone.

"Wait a minute." His voice struggled to control its temper. She knew Cozy didn't like to fight with her. But whenever they had a discussion of any sort; he had to have the last word—it was the one way he could convince himself that he was still the boss.

"I never said I owned you." He put down the bottle and dried his fingers on her last clean towel. "But I have faith in you, don't I?" He turned her around and looked at her with that earnest expression that you could almost believe was sincere.

"I have faith in me too," her voice challenged him quietly.

"The way you carry on. Who else was ever so good to you? What is it you want that I don't get for you?"

She looked around the tiny dressing room and snorted. Her four dresses hung on an outside rack because the closet wasn't deep enough. She supposed he meant the convertible that he bought her when he thought she was dating someone else.

"Yes, you're good to me, Cozy. How about taking me home so I can get rid of this lousy headache?"

"Sure. Anything you say. I'll just sit here and wait while you get dressed."

He was all eagerness to please. Sarine grinned to herself with sour enjoyment, knowing that Cozy realized that his usual methods were about to backfire. He hadn't wanted to give her a contract when she started to work for him because he thought he could control her better that way—one false move and out she would go. Now, with her increasing popularity, he knew it had been the wrong move. She wouldn't have trouble getting a job anywhere. But he didn't dare ask her to sign a contract this late in the game.

While he sat patiently, Sarine brushed out her long hair and tied it into a neat dark chignon low on her neck. Then she buttoned herself into the simple dress of powder blue that made her look like a prude and a wanton all at the same time. The way this dress made men almost ashamed of themselves for staring at her always amused her.

"All right, Cozy, let's go." She picked up her purse and waited for him to open the door.

They passed through the dining room where chairs sat upside down on the tables. A silent, tired sound of a broom sweeping up stray cigarette butts made Sarine feel that strange letdown which always accompanied her home every night.

"Good night, Sarine."

She turned to see Paul gathering up his music. He stood in the shadows near his piano, tall enough to be the shadow of another man cast up against the wall. She wished he wouldn't wait every night until she left with Cozy. Paul gave her a strange sense of discomfort as though she were doing something wrong.

"Oh, Paul?"

Clearly she could see his face tilt toward her from across the room. For some reason she knew that face by heart. He had a way of saying things with his eyes and his mouth and his posture without the clumsiness of words.

Sarine stopped near the door and sent a smile to him over the tables. "Thanks," she said, "for the up-beat."

Then she stepped out into the night before he could answer.

The California sky had a way of making her forget that this was November. She got into Cozy's automobile and leaned back to search for the Big Dipper, enjoying the silent glitter spread out above. Soon, if she had any luck with Jerry Lutha, there would be no more warm skies like this in November. New York and bitter cold and slushy, people-packed streets. The prospect thrilled Sarine.

"If you've got such a miserable headache, what are you smiling about?"

She had almost forgotten Cozy. His voice didn't take the smile away. He was no more than a little fly buzzing around her life. She could swat him with two words if she cared to.

"Or maybe you're feeling better?" The hopefulness in his voice was pathetic. The great, swaggering Cozy hated to sleep alone.

"I feel rotten," she said truthfully. Her temples throbbed as though a grandfather clock were ticking inside.

"When we get to my place, you can stoke up on aspirin." He pressed on the gas pedal and the car shot up to seventy-five. Speeding was one of his ways of avoiding Sarine's objections. She didn't like to talk against the rush of wind.

The car nosed along beside the moonlit ocean that lay calm and flat, gently stroking the beach with a low swell of wave. Despite the pain in her head, Sarine felt as calm as the night around her. Very soon she would be leaving Cozy and so what difference would it make in her life if she slept with him tonight or if she didn't sleep with him? Lovemaking with Cozy was merely a ritual she performed without thinking.

She slid down low in the seat and continued to watch the stars. The car sped mightily but it couldn't catch the stars. Paul would know what she was feeling. Strange that they really knew so little about each other.

Cozy pulled up beside his house. Usually he put up the top and locked the car in the garage, but tonight he fussed over Sarine. Anxiously he held the door open for her. Then he took her elbow and led her up the side steps to the balcony overlooking the ocean.

"Sit down and rest yourself," he said. "I'll get you something." He stepped in through the French doors and snapped on the bedroom lights.

Sarine put herself in the chair and kicked off her shoes. If Cozy weren't in it, this would be the perfect house. After a night on stage, this isolation soothed her. No voices, no tense interlocked chords. Nothing but the impersonal sand blown by the roaming wind.

But Cozy returned, his heels clicking on the rubber tiles, making a sharp sound with their metal tips.

"Aspirin," he said, handing her a glass of water and a couple of pills. "Take them both. You'll be as good as new in a minute."

He picked up her shoes and set them neatly one beside the other. "I do treat you well. Don't I, honey?"

She swallowed the pills and his waiting hand retrieved the glass so she wouldn't have to lean forward to the table.

"Sure you do." And she wanted to slap him to get that little boy look of repentance off his neatly shaven face. Eager Cozy. Hopeful Cozy. Scared Cozy. Sarine knew that he must suspect something. He had an almost animal instinct for self-preservation—she guessed that it took the place of brains.

"I guess you did those things on stage tonight just because you weren't feeling well."

Let him search. Let him think he had the upper hand because she never lied to him.

"We draw a good crowd." She tilted the chair back and examined the moon. "Why don't you stop complaining?" If he were a man, she might enjoy fighting with him. But thrusting at Cozy was like kicking a starving dog.

He laughed nervously and loosened his tie. "We both need a good night's sleep."

True enough, but she didn't want to go inside with him just yet. No hurry to feel his arms around her, his hands on her body.

"Soon."

"Well, I guess I'll get undressed." His tone was part statement, part question.

"Yes, get undressed." She ordered him so that he would stop lingering around her.

The aspirin weren't helping at all. She knew how to ignore a headache. She knew how to ignore a hungry stomach and the scowls of agents who were sick and tired of listening to girls audition. She knew how to ignore just about anything that threatened to drag you down into failure. But she had these aching nerves because she knew that Jerry Lutha was one of the few people you just could not ignore.

What did she know about him, except that she needed his help? Some magazine photographs had pictured a sharp-nosed man with a receding hairline. Best of all, he was still young, maybe thirty-two at the most. He got places in a hurry. And he could get her places in a hurry too.

Behind her in the bedroom she heard Cozy humming a nervous tune.

Oh, what was the use in delaying it? She got up and sauntered inside.

He was padding around in the bottoms of his red and white striped pajamas. The drawstring flapped sadly from his watermelon stomach. She didn't like to look at him half undressed. He seemed so old and lost and hopeless in contrast with her own vivid life.

"Head better?" He came toward her and touched the buttons on her dress.

"So so."

Her body seemed to relax under the touch of his fingers, but actually she was still thinking about Jerry Lutha. Would he like Paul's music? Maybe she could swing a deal for Paul as well as for herself. It wouldn't hurt to do a few of his songs. She knew they were great.

Cozy had his arms around her and was pulling her to him. Automatically she leaned toward his body. She wasn't very tall but Cozy stood only a few inches taller and she could feel his frightened heart fluttering beneath the flabby chest.

"You like loving with me," he whispered, trying to convince himself. He smelled from a rose scented lotion that blotted out even the ocean's salty tang.

She allowed him to run his lips along her shoulder. The touch of his wiry moustache no longer made her recoil. The more she thought about Jerry Lutha, the sorrier she felt for Cozy. She had never felt sorry for him before, but now she could afford the luxury.

"You've got everything," she said, meaning money and greed and shrewdness. "You make out."

"I've got you," he said. "That's all I want."

Yet he must know what a poor bargain she was for any man. She gazed at his greased head and patted it with a sigh. Sarine didn't often think of herself in terms of love. She didn't have time. If she craved anything, it was the glitter of being on top of the ladder. Some people climbed mountains just because they were there. Sarine was climbing the ladder of success because it was there and she had to.

"Come on," she said gently. She stepped out of his reach and walked over to the mirror. The three way reflection could find no flaws in her perfect body.

"Well, go on," she said, as he hovered beside her. "I'll be with you in a minute."

Obediently he went to the bed and sat down on the edge of the mattress.

Looking at herself in the mirror Sarine considered how this body of hers very seldom worked itself into a sexual passion. One would think that this ripeness was made for loving, but how often she had to pretend an excitement that refused to kindle.

She did not feel sorry for herself. Just mildly curious. Of course she could hardly expect to become aroused by something like Cozy. Yet what kind of a man would arouse her? Idly she considered that it must be pleasant to abandon yourself occasionally. She didn't smoke because of her voice and she drank only rarely with the customers because she couldn't risk getting drunk. All the simple pleasures that most people took for granted seemed to have no place in her life.

"It's getting late." Cozy's voice was impatient.

"Oh, relax," she said, feeling a slight tremor of irritation.

She needed to be by herself this evening. Every so often she liked to get her thoughts together and line them up. She had learned early that a person goes in the direction of his thoughts. If you let them get out of control, you get out of control too.

Tonight, on the brink of her big try for Jerry Lutha's approval, she needed to organize her thoughts for the best possible advantage.

"Your headache will come back," Cozy ventured, tearing matches out of a matchbook and striking them one after the other. He would have lit a cigarette, she knew, except that it might give her an excuse to delay even longer.

She disliked knowing every twist that his mind took. She wanted to know only her own drives and hopes. Awareness of the drowning struggles of other people made her nervous.

No use trying to snatch a little privacy. She might just as well go to Cozy and get it over with.

She flicked out the light. With the darkness came fresh awareness of the surging ocean. She thought how good it would feel to swim naked in the icy water.

She climbed into the opposite side of the bed from Cozy, knowing that he wouldn't give her the benefit of sleep without possessing her first. Her headache didn't really concern him. She lay on her back and waited for him to roll over toward her.

She didn't have to wait long. The sound of his breath came from between closed teeth. She knew he did this on purpose to make him seem beast-like.

Automatically she dug her nails into the skin of his back. Not hard enough to break the skin, but deep enough to make him feel she needed him. His desire spiralled around her and he clamped her body in a bear-like grip. Blustering obscene words so that she would know what a man he was, Cozy took her for the few seconds that his weak body required.

When it was over he looked at her and she saw the yearning in his eyes for a few good words. Drops of perspiration glistened on his moustache and she wondered for the first time how Cozy would get along without her.

"You're all right," she said and wiped his moustache with a tissue from the bedside table.

And he probably was all right, she thought. She could name at least three other women who would be glad to take her place in Cozy's affections.

"Are you all right?" he asked.

"Yes," she said, because he wouldn't go to sleep if he thought she would be sitting awake without him. "Go to sleep."

She let him put his head on her shoulder and snuggle against her, and in a few moments Cozy began to snore, tearing into the lovely murmer of the sea.

Sarine closed her eyes, hoping for sleep to relax her, but her thoughts churned wakefully. She opened her eyes again and watched the silvery squares of light on her toenails. She must paint those nails a special color for Jerry Lutha's benefit. And Paul would probably look at her as though she were crazy.

His silent diapproval irritated her. He behaved sometimes as though he thought he had superior knowledge of everything, walking around with a perpetually aloof, slightly bored look on his face. But get him away from that piano, and then what did he know?

Sarine realized she couldn't even venture a guess—she had never gotten him away from the piano.

She slid her shoulder carefully from beneath Cozy's head and decided that she couldn't think about Paul. The songs for tomorrow were set, the white dress was ready, and her hair would be fixed simply; that's what she should be thinking about—the performance tomorrow.

Through sheer force of will Sarine fell asleep, and in her restlessness she dreamed vague disquieting things. Unconsciously, she pulled the blanket up over her shoulders against the chill that came not from the night air, but from her own body.

Yet when she awoke to the blazing sun, she bounced out of bed full of exultant energy. She found a bathing suit in the closet and ran down to the beach for a quick swim. The water cleared her head and sent sparkles through her body, priming it with good feeling and confidence. She swam briskly to clear the dregs of her poor sleep and then floated on her back, allowing the fingers of sun to stroke away the remnants of tension.

Breakfasting on the terrace, she allowed herself two poached eggs and a large glass of orange juice.

"Had a good night, eh?" Cozy said, watching her down the food. He crossed his ankles and lit a cigarette, regarding Sarine as though she were a prize animal.

She felt no need to comment about his sexual prowess. Towelling the damp ends of her hair, she wondered if Paul were at the club yet. He didn't know about Jerry Lutha and Sarine wanted him to know. You couldn't hit Paul by surprise and have him agree to everything already planned. He was the kind of guy you had to ask first.

Not that he would try to stop her. Paul would never get in anyone's way. But he could be very stubborn if you took him for granted.

Sarine threw the towel aside and went to put on some dry clothes.

"Hey," Cozy said. "What's your hurry?"

"I've got some numbers to rehearse," she called back, poking among her things in the closet.

"Well, wait awhile and I'll drive you over." He came inside after her like a pup that couldn't do without its master.

His pleading tone sent a burst of anger through her. Couldn't he at least pretend to one shred of pride? She felt like stepping on him and putting him out of his misery.

"For heaven's sake, Cozy, let me breathe!" She zipped up her dress and slammed the door of the bathroom shut behind her, glad to have some way of keeping him out of her sight for a few minutes. She put on some lipstick, hardly taking care with the movements. All she wanted was to get out of there, put some space between them. She felt she had to have some room to breathe.

When she climbed in the car, Cozy didn't say a word. He knew better than to tamper with her temper. They made the trip to the club in complete silence, Sarine glaring straight ahead of her the entire way. When the car came to a halt in front of the club, Sarine flung herself out without waiting for him to open the door. In a moment she heard the car take off again, skid around a curve, and she opened the door to the club.

"Early today, aren't you, dear?"

Sarine's glance caught Anna setting out packages of cigarettes in her tray. She was a frail girl with pale red hair and a quiet disposition that made men overlook her and women pity her. But for some reason she didn't like Sarine and what little venom she possessed came out in her morning greeting.

Without bothering to reply, Sarine headed straight for Paul who was already doodling at the piano keys.

"Hi," she said. "Got a minute?"

"Sure," Paul answered.

"Not in here," she said. "Come on out back."

"Okay." He shoved the pencil behind his ear and walked outside with her.

She pushed aside a half-emptied container of coffee and sat down on the wooden step. He rolled up his sleeves and sat down beside her.

"Look, Paul, tonight's going to be a big night for both of us."

He didn't seem surprised. A mild curiosity showed in his eyes and Sarine noticed for the first time that they were green and not brown as she had thought.

"Go ahead," he said. "I'm listening."

"I didn't want to tell you before because I wasn't sure. Jerry Lutha is going to catch the show tonight."

"So?"

She didn't expect him to leap up into the air, but she had expected some sign of life from him.

"Well, doesn't that mean anything to you? Do you know who Lutha is?"

"Yes. I know Lutha all right." His words came in their usual slow and jogging pace. He took out a cigarette and lit one.

"I'd like to do some of your numbers, Paul." She couldn't understand why she was being so sweet to him, why she was handling him like a temperamental artist when she knew he wasn't temperamental at all. In fact, he was one of the most unchanging, almost emotionless people she knew.

"I appreciate that," Paul said. "But I don't think Lutha goes for Spanish type stuff. You'd be better off doing slow blues numbers if you want to impress him."

"Stop kidding me. You know your stuff's great. Don't you want to get anywhere, Paul? Don't you ever want to do anything except sit around this place and rot?"

Her voice went up and got louder.

"Sarine." Paul clasped his fingers and locked them around one knee. "I wish you could believe me. New York's nothing." He spoke as though she were the one who needed help and advice, not himself.

"So you've been there once or twice," she answered a little unsteadily. "What does that prove?"

"I'm not trying to prove anything. There's nothing to prove, Sarine." He smiled at her with the kind of good will that almost fooled her into believing they were agreeing about something instead of having an argument.

"Lots of people have their names on theater marquees," he continued. "And lots more make plenty of money. So what of it?"

With all the fury boiling inside her, she couldn't stay seated. She came to her feet and strode in small circles, her heels kicking up puffs of dust.

"Oh, what do I have to do to put some sense into you?" She folded her arms and stared at him. "If you want to act like a fool for the rest of your life, that's your business. I'm going to New York and live a little. But I'm going to peddle your songs in spite of yourself. Not because I have any feeling for you, you understand. But because you have a great talent lodged, I'm sad to say, in a block head."

At last she saw some life spark up in his cheeks. A sudden flush suffused them with red. She stood smiling at him with triumph in her face.

After a moment's silence, Paul got up and tried to take Sarine's hand. She let him hold her fingers in his, conscious that he was ice cold.

"I'm glad you like my music." His face was far above hers and she had to raise her head high to see him. From this angle the bones of his chin outlined his face strongly. That strength didn't go with the soft voice. Nothing about him was relaxed, she realized suddenly, except his voice.

"But it's not enough for you to like my music."

She wanted to take her hand away and stop him from saying what she was afraid he would. But instead she stood there.

"Please, Paul..."

"No. Listen." He held her hands tightly so she couldn't pull away. "We've practically lived together for six months now. I've watched you work and I know that you're headed for the big time. It's just that you can't go on kidding yourself into believing that there's nothing else in life except plugging songs. You've got to realize that there comes a time when it's no fun anymore to go on doing things alone."

She didn't want to hear any more. He was talking pure nonsense and she hated to hear it coming from Paul.

"Don't," she interrupted him. "Please don't go on."

"I've got to tell you," Paul said.

"But I know what you're going to say. I'm not that kind of a woman, Paul. I never was and I never will be. There's only one thing in life I can love. And that's myself. Don't go for me, Paul. Please. I want to be friends with you. Anything extra would only ruin it."

Anna opened the screen door on its squeaking hinges.

"Need any cigarettes, Paul?"

"Yes, thanks."

She edged a package into his shirt pocket and closed his fingers back around the quarter on his palm.

"On the house," she said.

Paul thanked her politely but it was obvious to both women that he really wasn't paying any attention to Anna. She let the door close with a bang and disappeared

"There must be something I can say to you that'll change your mind." He searched her face earnestly. "Or at least make you think about all this again."

"I know myself, Paul. Don't you respect that?"

"It's not a question of respect," he persisted. "You're human just the way everyone else is. You can't grow all by yourself and not miss all the so-called normal things that people do."

"I guess there's no point in going on like this," she said. Her voice was calm now. "We just don't speak the same language, Paul."

He took out the package of cigarettes and peeled off the cellophane.

"I'm sorry," he said.

"So am I."

She looked up at his face and felt a rush of sadness. Outside of this one thing, she knew, they had nothing else to argue about. They had so much in common—and yet, because of this single difference, they could share next to nothing with each other.

CHAPTER TWO

IT WAS eight o'clock. Sarine stood out of sight in the wings, waiting for Paul to start her introduction. He must be feeling the excitement too, she thought, watching him play special chords to soothe the restless audience.

But Cozy didn't look pleased to see the house packed so early. She saw him wedging a zig-zag path between the tables, heading toward her.

"See what you did?" His tense lips barely moved to form the words. "They're a pack of animals."

Sarine nodded, feeling the delicious tension. One wrong move from her, one minute too long of boredom, and they would shout and smash. She had to keep them on the fine edge of interest for four hours; the thrilling challenge made her taut and ready with suspense.

As Cozy muttered unhappily to himself, Paul played the chords of her first song and Sarine glided on stage.

"I cried for you. Now it's your turn to cry over me…."

She saw their faces straining toward her and wondered if this was the way a lynch mob looked to its victim. But only Cozy was frightened by it. She toyed with this mass of expectation, first flattening it into calm, then lifting it into small points of interest. Sarine led audience emotions wherever she wanted them to go. And Paul carried her voice deftly on a bed of harmonic rhythm.

As the hours flew, Sarine felt herself growing more and more powerful. This was her real life, these were the moments that made the Cozys, all the mess and discomfort in the world bearable. The years of scrounging could be forgotten. She stood on the pinnacle of her music, commanding the people below to do as she wished.

Her willing subjects obeyed every desire. No sounds of abuse came from them now. They reflected each tempo change, responding with smiles or wistful looks or tapping feet. Half drunk, aware only of Sarine's voice, they swayed and sprawled and ogled like robots who could not think.

Occupied with her game and the prey, Sarine hardly noticed Jerry Lutha standing at the back of the room.

In the middle of a song, she spotted him. Standing aloof, he surveyed the audience before he even looked at Sarine. Then he came along the side of the room, and leaned against the wall, hands in pockets, and watched Sarine.

She sang straight to him. All the years of training combined with her natural talent in a triumphant display focused on Jerry Lutha.

Casually he lit a cigarette and exhaled slowly.

Sarine lifted her hair and let it fall heavily over her dark shoulders. If only he would come out of the shadow so she could see his face clearly. But she knew he was too smart for that. He wouldn't give her the chance to play up to his own particular tastes. All she could see was the wiry body dressed in a dinner jacket that blended with the darkness.

In a flash of decision, Sarine decided to forget his presence. She whirled away from him and aimed her voice over the crowd of customers. With renewed energy, she began the first of Paul's songs. The quick, strange beat set her hips in motion. Her voice rose to a high primitive wail, then dropped to the shuddering deep notes that made her audience quiver.

Still Jerry Lutha remained in the shadows.

But he was there. He hadn't dismissed her.

On the crest of roaring applause, Sarine left the stage.

As she stood in the little alcove beside the platform, she became aware of her exhaustion. Her body felt like a husk emptied of all its living cells. In that instant she didn't care if Jerry Lutha lived or died. She collapsed against the wall and closed her eyes, feeling the floor rock beneath her drained body. She had done her best. There was nothing more she could do. The rest was up to him. So she might as well sit down.

Paul was waiting at the door to her dressing room.

"You were great," he said.

She shrugged and managed a wan smile for him. He patted her elbow with reassurance.

"Your songs are what's great," she said finally, not wanting to talk to him or anybody else. She wanted only to be alone so that she could lie down and sink unobserved into oblivion.

She let Paul come into her room. He knew better than to make talk, and Sarine knew she didn't need to give him an explanation for this aftermath of depression. Paul as usual understood and in a moment left her. Relieved, she closed the door against the outside world.

The one fairly comfortable chair had two dressing gowns draped over the back. She pushed them to the floor and dropped into the seat. The small fan on the dresser looked at her helplessly and she looked back at it, thinking that maybe it would go on by itself if she concentrated hard enough. The dress felt too tight across her ribs and she wished it would just pop open. Everything around her seemed muffled and quiet with a deathlike silence. Was this the same dressing room she came back to every night? It felt so airless and tiny and unclean.

A knock at the door, and then Cozy's voice said, "Miss Duvalle?"

Oh, what the hell was he being so formal about? Then Sarine's mind clicked into action. She smoothed her hair and crossed her legs into a more graceful position before she called, "Come in."

Cozy entered with a flat artificial smile across his face. Jerry Lutha was behind him.

Sarine hardly listened to Cozy as he made the usual introductions. Instead she seemed to be hearing the peculiar sound of sparks flying between Jerry Lutha and herself. She had never been looked at quite like this. His eyes were two dynamos of electric blue; their sight churned through the layer of surface details and reached the essential core of what made Sarine.

"I enjoyed your work," he said blandly, but the words were clipped and sure.

Cozy took out a gold knife and elaborately cut the tip off a cigar. "The Jingo Club spotlights the best," he said, but his words did not interrupt the electric tension that passed between Jerry Lutha and Sarine.

"I hope you enjoyed the Spanish songs," she said. She wanted Paul to get some credit, but she knew also that it would be more effective to shift the praise away from herself. Yet falseness would fail on this man, she recognized; those eyes would spot a phony instinctively.

Sarine watched him as he stepped back from the cloud of smoke Cozy was fuming and took a cigarette case of brown alligator out of his pocket.

That's my man, Sarine thought.

Jerry Lutha was the other side of her gold coin. With her talent and his knowledge, they could raise a fire in New York that would burn to the skies. She didn't smile now and she didn't try to be charming. A strange peace crept through her tiredness. Here at last was a man—and a life—that she had always wanted and for which she had always fought.

"Oh, yes," Cozy said anxiously, trying to break up this puzzling intimacy. "You'll want to meet Paul Forde. Talented boy, Paul. He's got a stack of new music you'll want to see. This was only the beginning."

"Of course."

Watching this man, Sarine could tell that he couldn't be less interested in Paul's music, and she felt a twinge of disappointment.

"Paul's music draws the customers," she offered, hoping for a more enthusiastic response.

Lutha smiled at her, obviously amused. "I'm sure. The way you put it across has nothing to do with it, naturally." The nostrils of his sharp nose widened with his polite smile. By no means was he a handsome man. But his polished masculinity made him terribly attractive.

Sarine handled his compliment delicately. Her years of self-confidence were beginning to pay off now. She could afford to stick up for Paul, and she was sure that her judgment of the music was right.

Cozy said, "If you'd like to come out and meet him..." He couldn't finish the sentence because neither of them was listening.

"Frankly, Miss Duvalle, I'm interested in you."

He came forward and looked down at Sarine, his eyebrows drawn together in a line of no-nonsense. "Would you like to come East and try your talent in some of the clubs there?"

"Try her talent?" Cozy tugged at his vest with indignation. "Miss Duvalle doesn't have to try her talent anywhere. She has a perfectly fine place here." His voice floundered at Jerry Lutha. "Nobody orders her. She draws up her own shows. Who would be crazy enough to want to trade all that for a winter in New York?"

"I can speak for myself," Sarine offered in a low tone.

Cozy turned to her with that look of helpless appeal she loathed. "You want to be a little fish in a big pond?"

"Why not a big fish in a big pond?" Sarine gazed at her ankle bone while she listened to Jerry Lutha chuckle.

"You're tired, my dear." Cozy's tone was violently gentle. "Why don't you sleep on the idea? I'm sure Mr. Lutha will get in touch with us in a few days and we can discuss this further."

"If you don't mind, I'd like to speak with Mr. Lutha alone for a few minutes."

"But—"

Sarine watched him stand there, wordless. He must be thinking of all the things he couldn't say. That she had a contract to fulfill, obligations. So where do you stand now, Cozy? What has happened to all your shrewd schemes for making me dependent on you?

"Please," she urged gently, not wanting to see him crumble in front of her.

She continued motioning toward the door until he had backed out.

"Will you close it, please?"

Lutha flipped it shut, then pulled up a straight back chair near Sarine.

"Now," she said, not bothering to disguise her businesslike attitude.

Lutha studied her for a second and Sarine realized how many lines cross-patched his skin. The illusion of his youth disappeared at close range. She wondered what he did in his spare time—if he allowed himself to have any spare time.

"He's not going to release you," Jerry said bluntly.

Sarine took the stub of his cigarette and put it out in a small copper ash tray that Paul had made.

"There's nothing to release. No contract. Nothing."

"Somebody was either very clever or very stupid." He glanced at her nails. "You should use an irridescent polish when you're this tan."

"I will if you say so." She smiled comfortably and pushed off her shoes.

"Here's the point, Sarine. You've got terrific delivery and a feel for audience response that lots of singers would give their eyes for."

She smiled, enjoying the compliment and his using her first name.

"Your voice isn't so bad either. A little raw in spots but I think it adds zest. Don't change it. Don't get fancy. Your trump card is this animal thing you put across so well without getting actually lewd. Old men who can't get a rise, the rough and ready boys who have seen it all—they're your ready made audience. No sweet stuff. No teen agers. You'll never make the hit parade. But there's lots of money elsewhere."

"At least you're honest." It was a strange thing to feel that she could undress in front of this man and he wouldn't even notice that she was a woman. The idea disturbed her. She couldn't decide whether this w something she liked or not. Sarine always counted on her body to put across what she couldn't say with words. Now here was a guy who treated her in an almost man-to-man way. She felt as though something had been taken away from her.

"Honest? I can't afford not to be." He cracked his knuckles. "More steady cash being honest. Saves time. Saves heartache."

"Is money all that you think about?" She knew it was a stupid question.

"In business, what else is there?"

"Kicks, maybe."

She realized she was sounding like Paul. This was hardly the time to be acting like Paul.

"This is a hard, back breaking, heart tearing way to earn a living. If all you're looking for is kicks, maybe you'd better stay here."

She sat forward with a sudden desire to make him understand.

"You know better than that," she said. "You know very well what I want or you wouldn't have bothered to stay for the whole show."

"I can be wrong sometimes."

"You're not wrong now. You think you came here tonight by accident? I went to Los Angeles four months ago to try to meet your cousin. If you knew how many somersaults I've been turning to lure you down here somehow, you'd know I wasn't in this thing for kicks."

She relaxed against the chair and let a long sigh escape her lips. He liked honesty. Well, she'd give him all the honesty there was.

"Let's face it—you're not telling me anything that's news."

They looked at each other and laughed.

While Jerry smoked another cigarette, she went behind the screen and changed into a skirt and blouse. What tickled her most of all was this new sensation of having a friend. She had never lived in one place long enough to make any real friends. Competition was what she thrived on and most of the people she had known weren't interested in show business. Maybe it was her aloneness which made sleeping with people like Cozy bearable. And she felt Jerry would understand.

As she smoothed the ends of her blouse against her slip, she decided to ask once more about Paul. Maybe he didn't want to commit himself in front of Cozy. Perhaps Jerry had thought that the idea of taking both herself and Paul away from the club would be too big a bite on Cozy. That's if Jerry had a heart.

"Tell me something," she called over the screen.

"I'm listening."

"You did go for Paul's music, didn't you?"

She heard him jiggling the ashtray on her dresser. The metallic sound of impatience took the place of words.

"Well?" she persisted.

"What is it with you and this Paul?"

There was no jealousy in his voice. Only a simple request for understanding.

Sarine came out fully dressed and pushed the ashtray out from beneath his finger.

"I just happen to think his music is tops, that's all."

He met the challenge in her eyes with friendly resignation.

"Okay," he said. "The songs were wonderful, magnificent. Genius."

"Why are you making fun of me?"

"I'm not. You're entitled to your taste. If you go for his brand of music, enjoy yourself."

"You don't?"

"I'm sorry. As far as I'm concerned, people like Paul come a dime a dozen."

Sarine turned away from him, not wanting Jerry to see the anger burning in her cheeks. He was not right. She knew music. She was as much a judge as Jerry Lutha.

"You're a gambler," she said. "Since you're gambling on me, why don't you take Paul along for the ride?"

He turned her around and smiled without sympathy, without kindness. "Give up," he said. "Save your own skin and be glad. You've got plenty of tough going ahead of you without carrying him on your back. I could understand it if he were your husband or somebody . . ." He looked at her with question.

"Of course he's nothing to me personally." She watched to see if her disgusted tone was strong enough to erase his doubt.

"Just the music?" Jerry persisted.

"Just the music."

"Then a smart kid like you should have enough brains to call it quits."

The hardness in his voice was unrelenting. She realized that without this bloodless realism, Jerry Lutha could never have gotten to where he was. Instead of fighting Jerry, she ought to go along with him. He was giving her more patience and attention than she, as a stranger, deserved.

She went to the mirror and smoothed down her eyebrows. "Okay," she murmured. "You're the boss."

He slid away from the topic to ease her out of any embarrassment.

"Look," he said, "I'm going to be busy tomorrow and Sunday. Supposing you get in touch with me at my hotel on Monday morning. We'll straighten out all the little details and make some solid arrangement."

She watched him scribble a phone number on the back of a card and drop it beside her purse on the dresser.

"Fine," she said. "I'll be there."

Without thinking Sarine offered her hand to him and he clasped it with a gentle pressure. The warmth of his skin sent a tiny thrill along her arm.

Without ceremony he left her to the seclusion of her cluttered dressing room.

But not for long. As soon as his footsteps disappeared, she heard the quick, clicking sound of Cozy hurrying to her. If she had any sense, she'd stuff her ears with cotton. She knew the routine he was going to pull. Why couldn't he get it through his head that she simply couldn't care less?

"Well," he said, sweating miserably and trying to look nonchalant. "Filled your ears full of big stories, didn't he?"

Must be nice to smoke, she thought, so you'd have something to do with your hands to keep them from reaching out and poking little pests in the nose.

"Fairy tales about how he's going to make you a big star on Broadway. Wolves, all of them. Trying to make out by sounding like big shots."

"Either lower your voice or shut up." She was feeling good, and she didn't want Cozy to spoil it. Later she would put up with his little act. But just this moment, she wanted all for herself.

"So now it's shut up, is it?" He flopped down into a chair and extended his feet with possessor's privilege. "One word from some slick big mouth and now it's me who should shut up."

The pain of his bravado made her shiver. Where was he getting the guts to act like this? Perhaps, in Cozy's heart and soul, he didn't believe that Jerry Lutha was serious about her. Maybe he didn't really think that she had enough talent for Broadway. His little frightened mind thought in dead-ends that began and stopped with Jingo Club.

But she wasn't going to argue with him. Tonight she would go home and sleep in her own bed all by herself.

"Say something. Go on. Give me an answer that doesn't sound like a kid who's being taken." He waited, hungry to pick an argument with her.

"Let's not," she said. She had no quarrel with Cozy, and certainly he had none with her. Of course she didn't expect him to be good enough to wish her success, but if they could avoid nasty words just for the sake of being civilized, maybe she could someday remember Cozy with a little affection.

"Sure, you don't want to talk," he was saying. "You don't want to open your mouth and watch yourself turn into a fool. I thought you were smart. You twist me into doing anything you say. But when it comes to the real thing, you're just another two-bit dame."

She realized he couldn't let her go without these last insults. She waited, watching the sweat which stood unnoticed in the folds of flesh that rolled over his collar.

"Is that everything?" she said, forcing her patience.

"No," he said, warming up to his apparent success. He would not stop until he was convinced that he had won.

"Get it over with," she said. "Let's have it all out so everybody can get to sleep."

She had not wanted to stir him up, but she felt her own temper uncoiling. Folding her arms, she glowered at him. "Go ahead," she said, and her voice dripped with contempt and derision, "Everybody outside enjoys the show you put on."

"No-good slut." He fumbled out of the chair and raised his arm to slap her. But he stopped the action in mid-air. His hand began to tremble. "You can't leave me." He lunged and grabbed her to him. "I won't let you go."

She tried to twist out of his hold. The smell of fear came from him, revolting her senses.

"Stop it." She pushed at his shoulders.

His fists dug into the small of her back. "You can't leave me. I won't let you go."

She struggled against the increasing force of his hold. The pressure against her ribs stabbed with sharp claws of pain.

"Cozy, you're hurting me," she said.

He didn't hear her. His eyes, wide and frantic, were filmed over with his passion to keep her with him. She felt his lips roughly bruising the side of her neck, and the grip of his arms stopped her breath. She struggled against the bulk of his shoulder.

"Mine, only mine," he rasped.

She had to free herself. "Yes, Cozy, I'm yours. Please. Let me go. I can't breathe."

"You'll stay?"

"Yes."

"Never leave me." His arms cut into her sides.

"Never."

Slowly she felt his grip relaxing.

Pushing herself free, she stood away from him, watching with horror this creature who had become a pleading beast. His arms hung heavy and useless at his sides. The face, drained of all color, blinked at her with red-veined eyes that seemed hardly capable of rational thought.

"You'd better go home and get some rest," she said, feeling a nauseous pity for him.

"You're coming with me."

Sarine realized she should go to save herself more argument and further trouble. Yet she couldn't bring herself to face the thought of one more night with him. These last few minutes had filled her with a revulsion that she could not master. Earnestly she wished never to see Cozy again. If she starved on the streets, it would be better than to be in the presence of this thing that could not act like a man.

Knowing it was the wrong thing to do, she said, "I'm going back to my own place."

She started for the door, hoping to get to the safety of the now darkened Jingo Club. Just as she touched the knob, he grabbed her wrist and yanked her back toward him.

So fast that she could not see the motion, he began slapping her across the face. The stinging sensation brought tears up to her eyelids and his fingers turned into fists that pounded on her jaw.

Without thinking, she began to scream.

In a second the door burst open. Dimly she saw Paul yank Cozy away. She heard the ripping sound of material as the collar of his jacket tore downward. With a sickening thud, Paul's fist connected with bone and Cozy sank to the floor in a mass of quivering flesh.

Standing on either side of Cozy's unconscious body, they stood looking at each other. Paul's temper was something new to her. She watched it throbbing in the muscles of his jaw. His usual slouch had straightened out into squared off shoulders. Blood oozed from the scraped skin on his knuckles, but he didn't seem to notice it.

"Are you hurt?" he said in a voice she could hardly hear.

Her jaw felt as though it had been knocked out of place. "I don't think so," she said, touching the skin.

"You're going to be black and blue tomorrow."

She managed a laugh. "So what? I'm not going anyplace."

"I guess neither of us is going anyplace."

He took her elbow and led her gingerly around Cozy's stirring body. Like a child, she allowed him to guide her. She was almost glad for the mess with Cozy. Just to see Paul do something definite for a change somehow made it worth all the pain she had suffered.

"Let's go cool off," he said.

Obediently she followed him out to his car.

CHAPTER THREE

PAUL DROVE SLOWLY. Sarine listened to the squeaks and rattles of his car, thinking how very like its owner this uncared for automobile was.

"Don't you ever take this thing in for a check-up?" she said, pulling out the ash tray to discover it stuffed with butts.

"You're too particular," he laughed.

"Now honestly," Sarine persisted. "Wouldn't you like to have a new car every year and a wardrobe made to fit you and nobody else?"

"What do you want, my girl? Would it make you happier if I got down on my knees and worshipped at the altar of green like your new friend does?"

She detected something in his voice that wasn't the old placid Paul. There were lots of things she wanted to talk about concerning Jerry Lutha, but at the moment she was angry with Paul because Jerry Lutha didn't like his music. She knew it made no sense to take her own frustration out on Paul. But her disappointment overruled any ability to behave sensibly.

If Paul were the kind of person, she told herself, who kept up with the times and paid any attention to style and musical fashion, his music would appeal to Jerry Lutha. She felt herself blaming the entire situation on Paul's personality—or lack of it. Jerry Lutha was impressed by people who were confident and dynamic like himself; he wasn't impressed by Paul because Paul kept his personality and humor hidden away in corners. Of course Jerry didn't like Paul's music. How could he? A man like him could feel only contempt for someone like Paul.

"You're kind of quiet," Paul said. "Feeling okay?"

"I'm all right."

She didn't want to say the thoughts that were passing through her mind. They would only hurt Paul and for nothing. She had learned long ago that you can't change people. Either they changed themselves or they stayed just as they were. But the frustrating desire to open Paul's head and yell into it all the things she believed he should know for his own good was consuming her.

For awhile they drove on the road by the beach in silence. Lone cars parked on the sand told of other couples enjoying a different kind of silence.

"I wouldn't worry about Cozy," Paul said. The edge of concern in his voice argued with the words.

Sarine worked the ash tray out of the dash board and emptied it from the window. "Who's worrying about him?" she said. "Don't be silly. Cozy had himself a tantrum. He'll be over it by morning."

"Let's hope you're right."

She noticed that Paul sat rather stiffly with his back just barely touching the cushion. He seemed almost like an old maid aunt about to say "I told you so."

"And anyway," she said in an effort to clear herself of any guilt, "I'm not going back. Ever."

Paul didn't seem appeased. He kept his gaze steadily on the road. "Cozy'll find you if he wants to."

"Are you worried, Paul? Are you concerning yourself with that blubbering idiot who doesn't know which end is up?" This was a good topic through which to vent her irritation with Paul.

"If I were you," she continued, "I'd stop worrying about all the little ants on earth and get myself acquainted with what's going on in the bright world of people."

He found a cigarette but had no matches for a light. "Explain yourself," he said, crushing the unlit cigarette into the emptied tray. "I don't follow."

"All right," she said. "It's very simple. For your kind of work, you don't have to stay in a hell hole like the Jingo Club. If you knew the right people and gave yourself half a chance, you could be making twice the money."

"But you know I don't care about money."

"Well, how about prestige? Don't you care whether the people who hear you know that it's Paul Forde and not Joe Shmoo?"

She watched the yellow headlights picking out the white line on the highway in the darkness.

"Seems to me we've been through this before, Sarine. I'm not a mountain climber. I'm not even a hill climber. You can't expect me to change any more than I can expect you to give up whatever it is you're fighting for."

The finality in his voice left her no room for argument. Jerry Lutha must be right about Paul. And yet—and yet maybe there was something bugging him that he didn't want to talk about. In the back of her mind, Sarine had to keep room for an excuse. She couldn't sit back and label Paul a failure. He didn't look defeated. And he certainly didn't act defeated.

"We're just fighting for different things," he said, breaking into her thoughts. "Is that unforgivable?"

"Just as long as you're fighting," she answered, feeling relieved.

"Did you think I was sitting around like a dead fish on the beach?" he chuckled.

"How am I supposed to know what to think? You never talk about yourself. In fact, you never talk much about anything. What does anybody know about you except that you play the piano?"

"There isn't much to tell," he said, slowing the car and steering it on the sand. "I've been living up and down the coast for most of my life. No family to speak of. I was king pin in the Geller Home for Boys till I outgrew the place. Oh, yes," he pulled up the hand brake and stepped out on the sand, coming round to open the door for her. "I could brief you on New York since you're determined to go."

She left her shoes in the car, stepped out, and felt the coolness of the night sand against her bare feet. It occurred to Sarine that she should be terribly aware of this vast and balmy serenity. Perhaps in New York she would lie awake some night, trying to recall the silhouette of a palm tree or the pungent odor of seaweed drying in the line of foam.

Paul spread his jacket and helped her to sit down. Cross-legged he seated himself beside her and balanced his elbows on his knees, looking out toward the sound of the water.

"You have no right to make fun of me," she said, feeling not irritated, but sad that he did not share her own dream of success.

"But I'm not."

"Don't deny it, Paul. You think I'm crazy for wanting to go to New York. A star-struck kid. That's what Cozy thinks, too. Maybe you're not really so very different from him after all."

"That's unfair." His voice cracked with a hurt she hadn't meant to inflict.

She suddenly felt angry and exasperated. What was she doing here anyway? She should be home in bed. Or making plans for her future. She was grateful to Paul for rescuing her from Cozy, but that didn't mean they should be sitting on a deserted beach, picking at each other. Just once, why couldn't they be together and enjoy themselves?

"I'm sorry, Paul. You know I didn't mean that."

"Forget it." He turned over on his stomach and propped his chin on his palms.

An awkwardness hung between them that she could not disperse. There was a definite strain between them now, almost an antagonism. Underneath the conversation, a battle seemed to be waging. Why were they fighting each other? What, after all, was there to fight about?

She lifted a handful of sand and let it run between her fingers. Never before had Sarine been in a situation where she could find nothing to say.

His voice broke the heavy silence. "I have no doubts that you'll make out in New York. Not with Jerry Lutha behind you."

"Why don't you like him?" she asked earnestly.

If Paul had an honest reason for not liking Lutha, she wanted to know what it was. Even if she didn't give Paul much credit for being a sharp operator, she felt that his insight was at least as good as hers.

"I don't dislike him."

She sensed that Paul was backing away from further argument.

"The only thing I dislike," he continued, "is that you'd rather talk about him instead of—"

The sentence went unfinished and Paul put his head down on his arm.

For the first time it occurred to Sarine that maybe Paul had never possessed a woman. She had no other way of understanding why he persisted with words that implied a feeling to which she could not respond. If Paul wanted to make love to her, why didn't he make a pass? He knew she wasn't spotless. He saw her go home with Cozy every night. Certainly he didn't think they slept in separate beds.

She had never handled a perfect innocent before. That a man could reach Paul's age without having experience shocked her. She examined the soft-shaven bristles on his neck and realized how tender his skin was. Perhaps she should do him the favor of letting him make love to her. It wouldn't mean anything and she liked him well enough to want to help. But if she were his first, he might fall deeply in love. She had no time to bother with that kind of an entanglement now.

As though she had spoken her thoughts aloud, Paul turned on his side and smiled gently into her eyes. Then with an impulsive movement, he sat up and pressed his lips to hers.

Before she could allow herself to feel it, Sarine pushed him away.

"Don't you see," she said, "that it can't be right between us?" She took his hand, searching for more words that would say what she meant without cutting him to bits.

"No, I don't see," his voice was dull.

"This may sound corny, Paul, but I like you. I want us to be friends. Always. It isn't easy for people to be friends who are as different as we are. If we were alike, it would be all right to go to bed and take a little fun wherever we could find it. But with you and me, we'd only end up hating each other."

He took his hand away and pulled her down beside him on the sand. She felt the cold sand against her body but it didn't matter. Whatever she could do to make things easier for him, she would be glad to do.

"You couldn't hate me," he said. "If I knew it would wind up like that, I wouldn't bother. The trouble with you is that you're afraid of falling in love. It might interfere with your plans."

She started to protest but his mouth came firmly down on hers again. Shutting her eyes tight, she tried not to respond. If she could lie in his arms passive and unyielding, he would need no further convincing that she wanted only to be friends.

Paul did not force himself upon her. His body seemed to coax her to give in to him. Against her will she felt a faint quickening of her senses. Yet she lay still, not wanting him to know this. She couldn't let Paul take her and then run out with Jerry Lutha. Dammit, why wouldn't Paul come to New York with her?

Roughly she pulled away.

"Why can't you write something else besides that phony Spanish music?"

Paul looked at her as though she had gone crazy.

"What's that got to do with this?"

"Love bores me." She didn't know what else to say.

He burst out laughing as though she were a child who had told an adorable lie.

"Who said anything about love? We're just kidding around the way everyone else does on this beach. Why don't you relax and enjoy it?"

The knifing in his voice told her that this time she had really hurt him. She didn't know what else to do. He had to know how she felt.

"I'm tired, Paul. Will you please take me home?"

She stood up and brushed the sticking sand from the folds in her skirt. There was no reason to go on like this with him. No matter how she tried to let him off lightly, she only got herself deeper into the mess.

He remained sitting, waiting to see if she had anything further to say.

The only thing for her to do was to walk to the car. She left him sitting there, to follow when he would.

In a few minutes he joined her.

"We're going to my place," he said grimly.

"Paul, don't drag this on. I don't want to fight with you."

He turned the car around and swung back on the highway, angrily pushing the car up to sixty so that they jounced and tore into the wind.

"Don't take so much for granted," he said. "I'm not going to rape you."

Once again he was making her feel like a child. He could twist her motives with one word so that she sounded completely ridiculous.

"We're going to my place because I don't trust Cozy."

Sarine smiled. With that matter of fact statement the old reliable Paul had returned. She could almost feel the way he had clicked off the lover's role and become the protector. It almost sounded as though a door had been closed.

Sarine didn't think that Cozy would try to make any more trouble, but it would be best to let Paul have his way about this. Since she didn't let him make love to her, the least she could do was give him the chance to feel that he could still take care of her.

They rode along in silence. Relaxed and comfortable now, Sarine watched the moon riding high behind a gray gauze of cloud.

"Beautiful night," she said, hoping to make a neutral field for conversation.

He glanced quickly upward at the sky, then back to the road. A sudden shift of the wind flapped his tie over his shoulder and Sarine pushed it back.

"Yes, isn't it," he said without conviction. "When I was a kid, we watched the sky from narrow windows and it always felt as if we were missing something going on just past what we could see."

"I used to be afraid of lightning," Sarine offered, surprised to remember this. It had been a long time since she had been afraid of anything, yet she remembered her terror vividly. She also remembered that in a way it had been fun to be afraid. The fear made her so aware of being alive and of how precious life really was.

They came into town and the strong light of street lamps dispelled the echo of memory. The deserted streets made the small town seem even smaller. The car's motor sounded very loud as they passed rows of empty stores. The awnings flapped at the night wind in a seeming effort to pull free of the ropes that held them.

Sarine looked up at the darkened windows above the stores and she considered how the people behind those curtains lived a routine life that she had never known. Perhaps it was good to be awake every morning at seven and asleep every night by twelve. But she would never do it. How good it would be to live in New York where something was always happening, where life moved at such a fast pace that you would never be left alone with the eternal night that could make you feel so small and unimportant.

Paul parked behind a vegetable truck, led her down a front walk that cut a neatly mowed lawn in half, and then up the steps of an old boarding house where a worn-out sofa squatted on the porch.

He opened the screen door and she followed him along the carpeted hallway to a back room. The door wasn't locked. He turned on the wall light and she saw a small room simply arranged with a few pieces of maple furniture. She had expected it to be a place of disarray and comfortable carelessness. Instead she saw neat piles of magazines, stacks of sheet music in the bookcase and half a dozen pencil stubs on the dresser. No shirts or underwear betrayed his personal life. The white curtains and bedspread were newly crisp. Not even a pair of bedroom slippers poked out from beneath the double bed. And the night air filled the room with open cleanness.

"I hope you don't mind," he pointed at the bed, "sharing."

She sat down on the flowered reading chair which looked too small for a man of Paul's height.

"Not the first time," she laughed, without meaning the implication of her words.

He found her a pair of pajamas. Sarine accepted the top and tossed the bottoms back at Paul. She felt not at all hesitant about getting undressed in front of him until he said, "The bathroom's behind that door."

"Oh." Automatically she went in and started to take off her things. Folding her skirt and blouse neatly, she put them over the towel rack. As she released her body from the confines of her clothing, she became aware of Cozy's abuse. A large bruise stained the skin behind her hips, and a network of aching spread upward along her back. She felt suddenly worn and tired.

She could hear Paul, on the other side of the door, hanging things into the closet. His bare feet sounded cat-like on the linoleum. She wondered if he were feeling at all self-conscious or uncomfortable about her. But the suggestion that she stay had been his. She trusted that Paul knew what he was doing to himself.

She buttoned the pajama top and looked in the mirror to see that the material fell low enough to cover all vital areas. Satisfied, she put her underwear beneath her skirt and stepped back into the bedroom.

Like two children behind a barn they stood for a moment, inspecting each other's nakedness. Paul's chest and arms displayed a pattern of interlocking muscle unexpectedly solid and strong. She realized now why Cozy had fallen so heavily from Paul's punch.

"You look like an elf," he said.

She laughed and looked down at herself to see that the oversized jacket did not erase the curve of her ample breasts.

"Not a very graceful one," she said, wiggling fingertips that barely peeked out from beneath the cuffs.

"Come here. I'll roll up the sleeves."

Before she could take a step, he had approached her and was quickly folding the material back up along her arm. She noticed the dried blood on his knuckles.

"How does your hand feel?" she said, while he rolled up the second sleeve. "Will it hurt your piano playing?"

"It's okay," he said. "Let's get to sleep."

He flicked out the light and they both stood looking at the large bed that waited for them.

She heard Paul's breathing and she heard her own. She would not stand there and make another mess of the situation. She walked to the bed, pulled back the covers and hopped in. The mattress gave willingly beneath her body and she stretched her legs with a grateful sigh.

Paul climbed in on the other side and she could tell that he was trying not to lie stiffly near the edge. He twisted and turned though, searching for a comfortable position that would not appear self-consciously rigid.

Waiting for the release of sleep to free her, Sarine listened to Paul folding the sheet over the blanket. He could not make the bed any neater than it was, yet he continued to seek out wrinkles and smooth them. Sarine closed her eyes and turned her back to him. She must go right to sleep. If she thought about Paul, thought about them lying there so close to each other, he would sense her disquiet.

She started to count sheep, but in her imagination she saw Paul's suntanned body looking strong and delicious. Her nostrils brought her the odor of him. An honest, male odor, newly bathed. No sweet lotions camouflaged his maleness.

The air had begun to take on a pre-dawn chilliness and she snuggled deep under the covers. Lazily her mind reviewed the events of the evening. Her accomplishment with Jerry Lutha, the break with Cozy and her new closeness to Paul. After such a special night, how could she be expected to drift right off into sleep? She heard Paul swallow and knew that his mind was no less busy than her own.

"Paul?"

"Hm?"

"What are you going to do about a job?"

She heard him take a long breath and expel it slowly. Had he expected her to say something else? Something more intimate?

"Go down to the union, I guess. They always come up with something."

She turned and looked at his head on the pillow. The soft hair fell over on his forehead, curling just enough to make him look very young. The moonlight touched his eyebrows and she noticed how well-shaped and fine they were. There was nothing coarse or disturbed in his features and she knew that his emotions lay inside him in a secret, unexplored lair.

"As long as you're out of work anyway, why don't you come to New York with me? Just for kicks."

"You don't give up, do you?" he chuckled softly.

She watched him cross his arms under his head. The silhouette of his eyelashes made them seem very long. He looked now like a musician, a man with a sensitive, artistic temperament that needed to be cared for and nurtured. Sarine felt a wave of tenderness for Paul flow over her.

"No, I don't give up," she said with good humor. "I don't think it's ever right just to give up."

"Well, neither do I."

He had promised not to try make love to her again, and if he made a move toward her, she would remind him of that promise. But if she didn't want him, why was she talking her fool head off instead of going right to sleep?

She waited for him to reach out and touch her, planning what she would do and say.

"You're very quiet," he said. "No more arguments left?" His tone was good-natured.

"I'm sleepy." She was violently tired but the presence of Paul beside her prevented her from being sleepy.

"Then why don't you go to sleep?"

"I don't know," her voice trailed off.

"I know," he said, and shifted his body slightly.

Her body tensed. He was going to touch her with the strong softness of his huge fingers. More than a foot of space separated them, yet her skin tingled as if their bodies were already in contact.

"I know a lot of things," he continued, still looking up at the ceiling.

"For example," he went on, "I know that you're scared to go to New York alone. Don't bother to deny it. Damned good thing that you have some kind of self-preservation."

"You're being ridiculous," she said firmly.

She wanted Paul to go on talking and take her mind back from the precipice of sex to which it had wavered. She wasn't fool enough to deny that it might be joy to hold Paul in her arms.

"And another thing," he said. "You don't want a man to throw himself at you. You want to do the chasing. That's why I'm not going to touch you, Sarine. I'm going to wait until you make up your mind that you want me—or that you need me. Maybe it's the same thing."

She was glad that it was too dark for him to see her face. The skin across her cheeks burned furiously. What right had he to judge her feelings?

"I never saw such an overgrown ego in all my life," she whispered, desperately trying to save herself from further discovery.

"Nice, isn't it?" His laugh stroked her with friendly playfulness.

"I think it stinks."

Beneath her anger was the insistent urging of another need. She could turn over and make love to him so that he would never forget her. She could give him one unforgettable night, laugh and walk out.

Toying with the idea, Sarine edged closer toward his body. She had wanted to be very kind and generous with Paul. But now he deserved whatever he got.

She reached out and touched his earlobe. She ran the tips of her fingers down along the side of his neck.

"Want me to come to you?" she said in a small and fragile voice.

Paul didn't move toward her. But neither did he turn away.

She breathed lightly into his ear and rested her lips on his cheek.

"Maybe we should have some little thing to remember us by," she whispered.

Despite the cool insinuating tone in her voice, Sarine could feel her own heart beating birdlike and wild. She could sense the ruffling of her nerves, and her skin prickled down the length of her spine.

"Paul," she said. "Paul." Her voice had become rough.

He placed one arm around her shoulders and pulled her body away from his.

"Now, get this straight and don't ever forget it," he said. "I'm not a toy, and I'm not a robot. You're the most terrific thing I ever came across, but that doesn't mean you can swing me around by my tail. Or that you can get me to live your way." He kissed her swiftly on the mouth.

"You're a spoiled kid with a lot of talent," he went on. "I love you, Sarine. I'll probably always love you. But I won't fall at your feet. If there's going to be something between us," he said, "I'll make the rules." He kissed her again.

She lay breathless in his arms. Her mind spun dizzily. No sensible thought remained to anchor her to the earth. For one instant she thought about giving up New York and spending the rest of her life right here, insanely happy, in Paul's arms.

"And one last thing. You're going to New York, all right. I want you to get fed up with success, so fed up that it comes out of your ears. Otherwise I'll never hear the end of it."

As he said New York, she snapped back to reality. For one moment she could have been Paul's, but that moment had passed and she felt far away from him now. The craziness that had gone through her head belonged to another person.

She took Paul's hand off her shoulder.

"You made a mistake, Paul," she said evenly. "You could have had me if you had been smart enough to take me then. But Sarine doesn't love anybody but Sarine. Scared or not, I'm going to New

York. And I won't get fed up with success." She turned her back to him and pulled up the blanket. "I'll thrive on it."

Neither of them said another word. Drained of all her energy, Sarine fell asleep at last.

She dreamed of footlights and spotlights and newspaper headlines in *Variety.* Warmly, success swathed her in its lovely cocoon. The sound of millions of hands applauding touched her with ripples of approval.

When she awoke Paul was already dressed. Slouching in the chair, he was making notations in a book of music paper.

"About time," he said, sliding the pencil behind his ear. "It's almost noon."

"About time for what?" she replied. "No rehearsals today, dear."

Nothing of what happened the evening before colored the beautiful morning. Sunlight splashed gaily about the room. She turned and rolled around the bed, feeling the warm sheets rubbing against her exposed skin.

Holding the pajama top down, she swung her legs carefully over the bedside, to the floor.

"I'm hungry," she said. "Let's go have a fat breakfast."

"Wonderful," he said, tossing the book on the dresser. "We'll make one last big day of it."

The sunlight fell across his eyes as he smiled kindly at her. She hoped that in the back of his mind he wouldn't hold what had happened against her. She wanted to remember Paul with affection, but even more she wanted Paul to remember her the same way.

As she turned on the faucets in the bathroom, she heard a small knock on the door.

Paul said, "Who is it?"

From the other side a muffled voice said, "Anna."

"Can you wait a minute?" Paul said. "I'm not quite dressed yet."

"Of course," she answered.

Sarine opened the bathroom door and looked out at Paul.

He raised his shoulders in an expression of embarrassment.

"Let her in," Sarine said. "What are you afraid of?"

A pained awkward look made him squint at her. He started to answer, but changed his mind.

Sarine left the door just slightly ajar and Paul let Anna into the room.

"Hi," Anna said. "I missed you at the drug store. Just came by to see if everything was okay. When Paul Forde misses breakfast—"

Sarine, fully dressed now, stepped out of the bathroom with the pajama top over her arm.

"Good morning, Anna." She smiled pleasantly. "How are you today?"

Anna looked at her and swallowed. Her pale face became even whiter. She touched her hair self-consciously and tried to smile, first at Sarine then at Paul.

Paul folded his arms and sat down on the bed. "We're just going out for breakfast now, if you'd care to join us."

"Please do," Sarine urged, adding a last touch of lipstick and trying to keep her mouth from spreading with amusement. She had never seen any one person at such a loss for words.

Anna cleared her throat. "I didn't mean to interrupt." A nasty smirk made her lips thin.

"You're not," Sarine replied. "Paul and I are just celebrating our last fling at the Jingo."

"I heard about that," Anna said. She looked at Paul for a second and then fluttered her glance down to the floor. "We're going to miss you," she said softly.

"Thanks." He got off the bed and came between the two women. "Well, shall we go?" he said gaily.

"No, Paul," Anna said. "You go on with—her." She opened her purse and took out an amber vial. "I'll just have a little water, if you don't mind."

Sarine and Paul watched as she swallowed a capsule.

Sarine knew that something must be ailing Anna to make her disposition so constantly unpleasant. Anna was the kind of girl who should be working in a bank or a quiet little store. She had no business working in a night club where the unhealthy atmosphere could so easily destroy her frail body. If she were stronger, physically, Sarine might enjoy a little cat fight with her now and then. But the girl seemed so weak and helpless that Sarine could feel only pity for her.

The three of them went downstairs and Anna quickly left them alone.

Sarine watched her walking up the street, her sheer green dress fluttering in the morning breeze.

"You two always have breakfast together?" she asked thoughtfully.

"Why not?" Paul answered, steering her across the street. "She's a good kid. Does my mending sometimes, takes my things out to the cleaner. A regular guy."

"I'll bet," Sarine replied.

It had never occurred to Sarine that Anna might be in love with Paul. The new knowledge made lots of little things fall into place. She understood now why Anna made digs at her for no apparent reason. The girl had a reason, all right; the best reason a woman can have. She thought that Sarine was keeping Paul away from her, and the episode this morning probably proved it to her beyond any doubt. Sarine almost wished her well. Anna would certainly be better for Paul than she would herself.

They sauntered into a luncheonette and found an empty booth toward the rear. Noonday lunch crowds made a noisy clatter of silverware. The waiter looked at them peculiarly when Paul ordered scrambled eggs for them both.

Sarine couldn't put aside her revelation about Anna. As she stirred sugar casually into her coffee, she said, "Ever take her out?"

"Anna?" Paul laughed. "No. Of course not. Why?"

"I don't know. She seems like a nice enough sort."

Paul unfolded the napkin and laid it casually across his knee. "Think I should start?" he said, a hint of amusement glinting in his eyes.

"Yes, I do," Sarine replied bluntly.

"Why do you care?"

"No particular reason."

The more she thought about Paul with Anna, the more Sarine became intrigued with Anna's jealousy. Now that she was going to New York, maybe Paul would start seeing her, even though he denied being interested.

"Stop beating the subject into the ground," Paul said finally.

Paul was right, of course. She had really no reason to think any more about the girl. She had no reason to think about Paul either, for that matter. Today and tomorrow she should not think about anything except having a good time. All she had left now were these forty-eight hours before Jerry Lutha would step in and take over in her life.

CHAPTER FOUR

SARINE KNEW THE name of the hotel where Jerry Lutha was staying, and Monday morning she caught the early bus for San Diego.

As the bus moved along, she felt herself hurrying toward a new life. The old troubles fell away from her. Already the Jingo Club was a memory from somewhere in the past. She watched the telephone poles whipping by. They seemed to be peeling off her old skin, leaving her fresh and newborn.

Not even Paul could cloud her happiness. She hadn't convinced him to come with her to New York, but she believed that he'd get to New York sooner or later—if he did love her.

The bus pulled into the terminal and she took a cab to the hotel. Perhaps it would be more businesslike to phone first, but she wanted to be certain that he wouldn't think twice about any lack of formality between them.

As she waited for the hotel clerk to inform Jerry Lutha of her arrival, Sarine looked around the lobby. She was accustomed to being the center of attention and here, nobody seemed to notice her. The women were every bit as well dressed as herself. She watched one stately woman walking toward the elevator. The woman bore her expensive look with the nonchalance that implied she had never known any other way of life. She could be fifty, she could be thirty. No lines on her face hinted of any thought that was more excruciating than that of what to serve for dinner.

Sarine thought briefly that this woman's husband might be in her audience some day, and the thought pleased her. It gave

Sarine a peculiar feeling of equality with this person who would no doubt have pity or even look down on Sarine's way of life.

The clerk said, "Miss Duvalle? Room 702. Take the second elevator on your right, please."

She nodded a thank-you and ambled toward the woman who stood waiting for the same elevator. They waited side by side and the woman gave her that impersonal smile which poised women sometimes exchange among themselves. No hint of jealousy reached across to Sarine and she felt glad that for once her good looks were not an obstacle.

The woman got out at the third floor and Sarine continued alone with the elevator operator to the seventh. She wasn't thinking of Jerry so much as how she would spend all the money that was about to come into her life. She had a lot to catch up with to balance out the years of doing without.

The heavy maroon carpeting muffled her steps as she walked down the corridor to Jerry Lutha's suite. One would think that the hotel was designed to protect the wealthy from anything that might jar the nerves into wakefulness. Sarine felt that she had stepped over to the far side of a rainbow.

She pressed the pearl buzzer and waited.

In a few moments the door opened. A stout little woman in a grey suit peered up at Sarine through tortoise shell glasses.

"I'm Sarine Duvalle. Mr. Lutha is expecting me."

The woman took off her glasses and let them hang on a chain around her neck. "Oh, yes. He'll be right with you. Why don't you come in and sit down?"

Sarine entered a large room that had been converted to an office. An old typewriter stood open on a table and letters were scattered all around it.

The woman scratched in her iron gray hair and smiled with that hurried, routinely friendly smile that told Sarine she had seen a million just like herself and wasn't impressed with any of them.

"Why don't you make yourself at home?" she said and pulled up her own chair behind the typewriter.

Sarine placed herself into a gray leather armchair that blended with the woman's hair and clothing as though she were the superior piece of furniture. The typewriter began to clack, barring any possibility of conversation between herself and Sarine.

Almost fifteen minutes went by before Jerry Lutha came out of his private room. Sarine waited while he walked with a bow-tied gentleman to the door. They were still involved in deep conversation and the gentleman had his arm around Jerry Lutha's shoulder, as though trying to convince him of one last point before reaching the outer door. She doubted that Jerry Lutha even saw her until he had said goodbye.

"Sorry to keep you waiting," he said and his voice sounded preoccupied.

Sarine followed him inside to the private office, feeling a twinge of disappointment that he had not boomed a smile at her and acted really happy to see her.

"How're you doing?" he said, closing the venetian blind that covered the wall length window. "How's your boy friend?"

"What boy friend?"

She watched him flick on the air conditioner and felt the room beginning to cool.

"Any boy friend. Don't you have a boy friend?"

She didn't mind the flip tone. It was the kind of thing she expected from a man who thought twenty-two was really very young.

"All my boy friends are fine," she bantered in return. This room, like the other, felt half business, half living. She wondered if there were any place in the world where Jerry Lutha did not take an appointment schedule and half a dozen letters along for consideration.

He sat down in a wing chair and regarded her. The receding hair seemed much thinner in the daylight. His fresh shave left a white blanket of powder on his chin. He looked somehow like New York. The completely relaxed position of his limbs indicated to Sarine that he probably never did relax. But his inspection of her was warm and charged only with good will. She sat very quiet under his scrutiny.

"I mean your piano player," Jerry Lutha said. "Did you bring him with you?"

Sarine returned his smile, making her own just as wicked.

"No," she said just audibly. "All I brought was me."

"You didn't give up on him already?"

"Didn't you say nix?"

"I did."

"So I left him home."

Jerry grinned and the laugh lines etched up to his cheek bones. "I don't believe you," he said.

"All right, so you don't."

She didn't want to talk about Paul. He seemed to be following her around like a bad dream. And she had hoped that being with Jerry Lutha would waken her.

"The reason I'm pulling your leg," he explained, "is that I don't want to find myself involved with a piano player when it's too late for me to defend myself." There was no malice in his voice. Just good-natured good sense.

Sarine waited while he lit a cigarette and looked around the room for a tell-tale photograph of someone. Men like Jerry often had a sentimental side. But her inspection discovered only sun glasses, cigarette lighters, and a variety of alligator pass cases scattered over the dresser and night tables.

"Let's forget Paul," she said.

Jerry crossed his legs, folded his hands over his belt, and leaned back. "Delighted to."

"There is no one important enough for me to miss when we get to New York." She had no reason to say this except she wanted Jerry to know how free she really was.

"Too bad," he said. "It's pleasant to miss somebody once in a while."

"Do you?"

"Sure."

She wanted to ask who, but she dared not pry. The muffled but self-important sound of the typewriter filled the silence.

He got up and went to a stack of papers lying face down on the dresser.

"Here," he said. "This is the usual contract that clients sign when they take on an agent. Read it over and see if there's anything you don't understand."

She took the papers and skipped quickly over the closely typed paragraphs.

"You're not going to cheat me," she said. "If you'll give me a pen."

"Don't be that way. Read it."

"And what will I know after I read it?"

"For one thing, you'll know that I'll practically own you for the next ten years."

She felt herself smile with that crooked grin that was her only remnant of bravado.

"It could be worse. What else?"

"Sarine, you're too trusting." He said it earnestly and with a hint of displeasure in his voice.

But why shouldn't she trust him? She didn't know how to start making headway in New York. She could put across a show, but that was all. The legal aspects of selling her talent were just so much Greek. He must know this.

"If I can't trust you," she said, "I might as well give up right now. You're Mr. Big, aren't you? Whatever you say goes. Why should I be the one to play smart? That's your business. All I can do is plug the songs. And I don't fool myself into thinking that's all there is."

Before he could answer, she took the pen and signed wherever there was a dotted line.

"So there," she said, pushing the paper toward him. "I'm signed, sealed and delivered."

He took the pen from her and put his own signature in the right places.

"This copy is for you," he said, handing the third copy to her.

Slowly she folded it and put it in her purse. She felt suddenly rich and instantly carefree. What could possibly happen to her now that wouldn't be good? "One of the kids in Jerry Lutha's stable—" that's how people in the business would refer to her. She felt proud and secure and happy.

"How do you feel?" he said.

"I feel like celebrating."

She had taken hardly any breakfast that morning. Half a doughnut dunked into a cup of black coffee was all that she had been able to get down.

"I guess you deserve a drink." He looked at his watch. "Maybe we both do."

"Bourbon and water," she volunteered.

He went to the telephone and dialed for room service.

She listened to the way he ordered, pleased with the easy politeness in his tone that did not make the servants feel like servants. She had been a waitress many times when bookings were scarce, and she knew far too well that there were very few people who didn't take advantage of this illusion of superiority.

It began to seem that everything Jerry did would only reinforce her trust in him.

He cradled the receiver and took off his jacket. "You don't mind?" he said, hanging it on the back of a chair and rolling up his shirt sleeves. "Maybe it's this weather you people have out here. Or maybe I just need to unwind." He went to the air conditioner and examined it to see if it could be turned up any higher.

Of course she didn't mind. The only thing that bothered her was that woman outside, who began to seem like some sort of spy. Sarine looked at Jerry's forearms and noticed how the hair curled on them, fine and dark. Certainly darker than what was left of the hair on his head.

"Californians know how to take things easy," she said. "It's an art."

"Maybe so," he said. "But I'd hate to have to crawl around like a snail in the name of art."

The outside bell rang and Sarine heard the typewriter stop.

The woman knocked on his door and a white-coated boy rolled in a tray with glasses and bottles and a silver bucket of ice.

To Sarine a drink was something that got sloshed at you. These embellishments that pursued the wealthy she would just have to adjust to.

Jerry signed the check and said to the woman, "You might as well go to lunch now."

Sarine felt pleased as she watched the woman control a snort. She obviously didn't want to go to lunch. She would have preferred to sit outside and guard Jerry from the fangs of this intruder.

But she didn't protest with words. She took her time, ordered the various papers on her desk, withdrew a purse from a drawer and walked out.

"I forgot to introduce you," Jerry said now that they were alone.

"I'm sure she'll be around," Sarine said.

"Oh, she's not a bad sort, Mrs. Reinhart. They get to be motherly at that age. It's good for them."

As Jerry poured their drinks, Sarine became acutely aware of some release within herself because Mrs. Reinhart had left. With the woman around, she had felt almost guilty of some unnamed crime. Now she stretched herself and ran her fingers through her hair and strolled around the rooms, sipping from her drink.

Jerry flopped into Mrs. Reinhart's chair and put his feet up on either side of the typewriter. "Someday when you're very very famous, you'll have a secretary who'll be just as protective."

"I hope not."

"But you will."

She smiled at him over the rim of her glass and wrinkled her nose with displeasure. "It's not nice for one person to know everything. But tell me more."

He took out a cigarette and struck a light from one of the books of matches on the desk.

"I'll tell you all the nice things," he said. "So you'll be happy for the rest of the day."

She sat down and waited for him to go on.

"You're going to have a huge bedroom," he said, "with a white bear rug and a little French maid. Every morning at ten-thirty you'll be awakened with a cup of tea in bed. And maybe raspberry marmalade on your toast. If you like raspberry."

"I prefer orange."

"Then orange. In the afternoon, you'll call me up and we'll talk about the best way to avoid paying all the thousands of dollars' worth of income tax because we'll both be very greedy. Of course, we'll figure it out to the satisfaction of all concerned and you can spend the rest of the afternoon dressing with a free mind. At six-thirty your chauffeur will call and drive you to the night club which is currently tops because you are appearing there and the owner will beg you to stay on for another three months beyond the length of your contract."

He was joking, of course, but the words coming from Jerry sounded very plausible to Sarine. She believed in him as though he were a magician of some kind. Whatever Jerry said, no matter how preposterous, was bound to come true. The alcohol was beginning to make her feel very light, and she could imagine no obstacles in her flight to success. If Jerry would simply touch something with the magic wand of his fingers, it would turn into whatever Sarine desired.

He got up from behind the desk and refilled both their glasses. Sarine laughed and clinked her glass against his.

"To everything we're going to have," she said.

He was standing very close to her and she felt again the fiery sparks from his deep set eyes. If he covered those eyes, she wondered whether he would still be as attractive.

"When is Mrs. Reinhart coming back?" she said.

"Not for an hour or so. Why?"

"I just wondered."

"You do a lot of wondering." He took her glass away. "You think very hard about all the wrong things."

She watched him put both their glasses back on the cart.

"What wrong things?"

"Like the piano player. And about when Mrs. Reinhart is coming back."

"I can wonder about other things too," she said. "Like when you're going to schedule my first appearance."

He nodded and put his cigarette out in a large crystal ash tray.

"We'll be able to get you an opening around the fifth of next month."

An arrow of concern shot through her. Next month. If she stayed out of a job for all that time, she wouldn't even have the plane fare to New York.

"A whole month?" she said.

"Nobody was prepared for the entrance of Sarine Duvalle," he said. "You must understand that a month is no time at all. Give me some credit."

The alcohol had dispersed whatever reserve Sarine had come in with.

"I thought you were a fast man," she said.

He touched his nose in an effort to hide the humor of another meaning to her words. "I am," he said and looked at her.

She didn't know anything about Jerry Lutha. Nothing at all. But who else was there in the world on her side? The strange flow of loyalty that she felt toward him did other and stranger things to her. She wanted Jerry to know how much she liked him. He was the other half of herself in a way she could not describe.

What did they share that drew her to him? The dynamic control of people might be a part of it. Their restlessness was certainly another part. Jerry could no more settle down to a routine kind of existence than she could.

"You're the kind of man one naturally expects to do things in a hurry."

His steady gaze wouldn't release her. Nor did she want to be released. She stood up and took a step toward him, hardly conscious of her action.

"And not only in a hurry," she continued. "But thorough."

"Why not?"

She put one hand behind his neck and drew herself up to him.

Because he wasn't a tall man, their bodies met almost like a pattern. She felt the flatness of his chest against the swell of her breasts, and his body was lean and hard and good against her own.

Sarine felt as though she had come home.

Her senses drifted away as Jerry returned her kisses. He wasn't going to lose control with her, she knew. The passion in his lips was a controlled fire. But this knowledge made Sarine abandon herself even more. As he ran his hands down her back, she shivered and, with a sudden burst of desire, bit his lip, unable to restrain the leaping need inside her. For days she had been perched on the brink of arousal and her body ached for release and satisfaction now.

Jerry made no move to take her to the bed. She wondered in a moment of irritation whether he was concerned about Mrs. Reinhart. Surely the woman didn't think that Jerry abstained!

Never had she yearned to be so close to a person. Whatever weakness she had, Jerry made up for. He was levelheaded without being a bore. He was shrewd but wise enough not to outsmart himself. He had position but didn't take a tyrant's advantages. If she could absorb his experience, his brains, his instinctive way of handling situations without trampling the little people—if she could become part of Jerry Lutha, maybe that would prove to be the goal she had spent her life searching for.

"We'd better take it easy," he whispered.

His good sense didn't cool her but she took her arms away from his neck.

"Save a little for next time," he said. And the way he said it was a compliment.

Sarine took a deep breath and pulled herself away. "Yes, boss man."

She stood still while he straightened the rumples in her blouse. His hands touched her with a careful devotion that was almost sexless. He wanted to groom her, to preserve her, to keep her in top condition for the important thing. And that's what she liked most about him. He seemed to know from the start where sex belonged in the scheme of their living.

"But not a whole month," she said.

"Why, are we back to that?" He had finished with her and was straightening his tie.

"Because—" But she didn't want to tell him she was broke. If he thought that she was beginning to depend on him like a child, he might lose some of his respect for her.

"Well?"

"Because I'm sick and tired of hanging around."

He smiled with sympathy. "I don't blame you. This one-horse town could drive even the horse nuts."

"Then let me come to New York soon."

He lit another cigarette. "You know I can't guarantee you anything."

"I'm not asking for a guarantee."

She was sure that once they were in New York he would exert himself to find her something good, and that he would succeed.

"I still say you'd be smarter to wait until I send for you. There are lots of odds and ends to be taken care of back East. You don't know half the work involved in something like this."

She wasn't interested. Her mind focused on one purpose. She had to get away from Cozy and she had to get away from Paul. She couldn't bring herself to go after another two-bit job just to keep herself going.

And the sooner she left for New York, the sooner Paul would realize that he wasn't going to convince her to do things his way.

"When are you going back?" she asked.

"Either tonight or tomorrow, depending upon whether or not I have to make a trip to L.A."

"Fine. I'll be there at the end of this week." All she had to do was figure out a way of collecting her back salary without getting Cozy angry. She didn't want another scene with him. It was so useless. But she couldn't go without the money. She wasn't the kind who kept a bank account for emergencies.

"You're nuts," Jerry said.

"That's possible."

"But I'm telling you there won't be any work available for at least another five weeks."

"And I'm telling you that I'm willing to take my chances."

He went to the appointment book on Mrs. Reinhart's desk and glanced quickly over the afternoon's schedule. "Have it your own way," he shrugged.

She straightened her seams though they weren't crooked and gave Jerry a flashing smile.

"Thanks," she said.

When she stepped out on the streets of San Diego a few minutes later, Sarine was almost bouncing.

CHAPTER FIVE

SARINE'S GOOD SENSE told her not to see Cozy again. Faced directly with his failure to keep her with him, there was no telling what he would do. Like a cornered rat, he might lash out without caring what hurt he might cause. Sarine wasn't afraid of him, but any damage done to her body could also do damage to her career. She knew this. And so did Cozy.

The hot sun combined with the whiskey in her system to make Sarine tired and irritable. She wanted badly to go somewhere comfortable and relax, but she knew no one in San Diego whom she could visit for the rest of the afternoon. As she walked further, the soles of her feet began to burn. Perspiration dampened her skin beneath the dress. She felt swollen and sticky inside her clothes. And her anger and annoyance about the situation with Cozy increased as she continued to think about him.

She bought an ice cream cone and found an empty bench in the speckled shade of a banana tree. If she could pull herself together, she felt certain that her mind would naturally lead her into the most tactful way of dealing with Cozy. The distasteful prospect spoiled her lovely mood of the morning. Jerry Lutha seemed so far removed from the bits and pieces of her present life; he stood untarnished and remote in the vacuum of her future.

Sarine was too restless to stay in San Diego until she had thought her problem through. Foolish or not, Sarine knew that she would go straight to the Jingo Club and have it out with Cozy.

The bus trip back dragged on and on.

Approaching the light blue building a few hours later, she gazed up at the neon sign, dead now in the daytime. She had never really considered the place apart from its night life. The surprise of noticing how old and worn the house looked made her stop at the roadside and consider. The paint seemed faded and dried out in the sunshine. A few of the shingles on the slanting roof were gone and should have been replaced by now. This, Cozy's investment, hardly resembled a well-kept darling. It puzzled her to understand how little attention he really paid to his business. Or was he scrimping in the penny-wise way that usually spelled defeat for puffed up and weak little men?

What difference. She had only to think of her salary. Cozy's welfare was the last thing to concern her now. She continued up to the front door and entered the cool shaded room.

"Welcome home, Miss Gypsy."

She couldn't see him, but she could tell from the thickness of Cozy's words that he was very drunk. His voice echoed through the emptiness and spilled its misery around her. Sarine took a few steps among the tables, looking for him.

"Over here, my dearest." A fist crashed down on the piano keys. "See? I can play too." With both fists now, he hit the keys, smashing out angry discords.

A film of disgust covered Sarine's annoyance. She could see him now, sprawled out before the piano. His sport shirt hung half out of his trousers. A stain of dried perspiration made a brown ring on the back. Disheveled hair hung over his temples and a shadow of beard grew in white stubbles over his chin. He looked very much older.

He swung around on the chair as she approached and his foot kicked over a bottle of whiskey that stood beside him on the floor.

"Doesn't your lover boy want you any more?"

She wasn't going to get involved in another scene. Maybe he had enough money in his pocket to pay her. She would take whatever she could get and leave. To hell with Cozy. To hell with his pathetic needs. It wasn't her concern—not his character, not his club, not his lost soul. She was through playing the mother act.

"Can you stand up?" she said.

If he would stand up, she would be content to take the money herself out of his pocket.

"Of course I can," he said. "But I won't. Why don't you pull up a chair and we'll do a duet?" He touched a few more keys and burst out laughing. "I can't get over it. Sleeping with Paul. Who in her right mind would sleep with Paul? Don't you know what his speed is? Cross-eyed high school kids. They go for him. They think he's wonderful. But I suppose you found that out."

So Cozy knew about last night. But that didn't surprise Sarine. Maybe Anna thought she could get back at her by telling Cozy. Both of them struck her as a pair of underprivileged bullies who couldn't get any enjoyment out of life unless they molested others.

She picked up the bottle and set it on the nearest table.

"You owe me a week's pay," she said. "How about it?"

"Money? So that's what you came back for." He slammed the top down on the piano. "You want to spend my money on that lousy bastard? That's what you think!"

"Are you going to give me what you owe or do I walk out right this second?" Her voice was low but level.

"Very scary. You're a very scary girl, Sarine. If I wasn't drunk maybe I would be crying. But you know what? I don't need you. What do I need you for? To give me trouble? Sleeping with that—I'll kill him. You just wait and see. I'll kill him."

His voice shot high and hysterical to the ceiling. He got up from the chair and wavered outward as though looking for Paul under the tables.

"All right, Cozy, you do that. But give me a hundred and a quarter or maybe I'll kill you."

"Go on, kill me. Put me out of my misery. You're not getting a cent, little girl. I'd rather be dead than watch you keep that jerk."

She didn't answer him. Instead she went behind the bar to the cash register and rang it open. She counted out four singles and threw them angrily back. No use. There wasn't any way of getting a cent out of him now. The alcohol gave him a kind of strength that he didn't have otherwise. The best thing would be to leave. If necessary, maybe she could borrow the money from Paul and send it back to him later.

"Go on," Cozy hiccoughed. "Scrounge for your quarters. The great, the high and mighty Sarine Duvalle, ladies and gentlemen, is flat on her face broke." He lunged behind the bar and opened another bottle. "Well, that makes two of us."

And now she understood why nobody was in the place. Usually by this time the waiters began to come in and set things up. But apparently Cozy had cut things short when she'd walked out on him. For an instant she felt a twinge of conscience.

"So long, Cozy," she said in a calmed tone. Then she walked out of the Jingo Club and didn't look back.

Now she had to find Paul. She walked a short way down the road and stopped in at the garage telephone. She dialed and waited. There was no answer. Maybe in her haste she had dialed the wrong number. She hung up and tried again. Once more no answer.

Was he with Anna? Could he be out looking for a job? The possibilities were infinite. And she didn't have enough time to go on a hunt for him. It would be best to go to his place and wait. She remembered that he left the door open.

The local bus took her into town. As she rode, it occured to her that perhaps he had left a message with her own landlady. When she got off, she dialed her place.

No, he hadn't called. He hadn't stopped by or left any message with her or her husband.

Of all the times for Paul to be out of reach. For the past six months he had always been at the tip of her elbow. Now, when she needed him, where was he? Between Cozy and no money and Paul off somewhere, Sarine felt ready to scream.

The walk to his house was just a short block from the bus stop and she almost ran the distance, thinking perhaps he had come home between the time she had phoned and now. The lack of food all day and the continuing tension showed in her appearance. Her hair tangled unnoticed on her shoulders and she had worked off the lipstick so that only an outline of her lips was left. But she wasn't thinking about these unimportant details. She had never come this close to a dead end before. Her mind worked furiously to find a way out of the predicament. She had to have enough fare to get her on the plane. She would worry about taking care of herself in New York once she got there. But now was the challenge.

She hurried up the steps to Paul's house and dashed down the short length of hallway.

She turned the knob and burst into the room. Her body went cold as she looked about.

The stacks of magazines were gone, and no music tablets filled the book case. She opened the top drawer of the dresser only to find emptiness. Quickly she pulled open another larger drawer. Only the newspaper lining there. She ran to the closet and threw open the door. Metal hangers swung rattling without clothes on them.

She sat down in the flowered chair and tried to understand what had happened. She heard the sound of slippers padding down the hall toward the room.

A little old man looked in on her.

"Did you want to rent this room, Miss?"

"Mr. Forde," she said. "I'm waiting for Mr. Paul Forde."

The man patted down the tobacco in his pipe and sucked on the stem.

"Oh, he won't be back, I'm afraid. Left sometime last night, I think. My boy wrote out his receipt."

"Well, did he leave a forwarding address?"

"Don't believe so." He took out a box of wooden matches. "I was just asking my boy what we should do in case Mr. Forde gets any mail."

She watched him move the flame in slow circles over the pipe. Puffs of sweet-smelling smoke floated toward the ceiling.

"Guess you can sit here for a little while if you want to," he said. "Awful pretty room, I think."

"Yes, it is," she said as he padded back down the hall humming a little melody around the stem of his pipe.

As she continued to sit in what had been Paul's room, an odd feeling of desolation came over her. Why had he run out on her? Unless he had left town altogether, what reason could he have for giving up this room?

Didn't all the months of their being together make her entitled at least to a goodbye? Or did he feel that what they had shared was so superficial that he didn't have to bother? She had never felt dismissed before. The sensation of uselessness overwhelmed her until she became angry in self defense.

Paul wasn't in the least open and free, she decided. He couldn't thrust himself at her and take whatever he got in stride. She had rejected him, so now he must be hiding off in a corner licking his wounds. It made her furious to think that Paul didn't have enough strength to fight back.

Well, she thought, then good riddance to him. Heavily she lifted herself out of the chair and left.

Sarine's living quarters looked very much like her dressing room back at the Jingo Club. Except for the bed and the other obvious pieces of bedroom furniture, the clutter of costumes, pieces of music and theatrical make-up gave the place a feeling of artificiality. One would have thought that the person living here was playing a game of make-believe.

Taking her dress off and slipping out of her shoes, Sarine looked around to see what she owned that could be pawned. Somehow among all this junk she should be able to raise enough money for plane fare to New York. The evening dresses alone had cost Cozy hundreds of dollars apiece.

She stuffed all the gowns that would fit into her valise, cursing herself for not having accepted any jewelry from Cozy in the early days of their affair.

In a moment she had put on a fresh dress, a pair of flat-heeled shoes and gone out the door, carrying the heavy valise.

The shop was half a dozen blocks down the street in what was considered the cheaper section of town. She had never had occasion to deal with this particular one, but Sarine was very familiar with pawnshops in other towns. Only since the Jingo Club had she been able to rely on the steady salary of a job. Her cast-off evening gowns were like a bank account that she kept for the rough times between jobs.

She pushed the door open and heard its welcoming jingle from a tarnished bell that hung on an elastic cord. Old guitars and knives and worn-out cameras hung on the walls and were stuffed in dusty show cases.

An old man looked up at her from above his spectacles and said softly "Good afternoon."

Sarine put the valise on top of one of the show cases and unsnapped the hooks.

"What'll you give me for everything?"

He watched her take the dresses out and spread them along the glass top. He didn't commit himself to any kind of curiosity and waited until she had completed her display before he even looked at the gowns.

"We don't have much use for evening gowns around here," he said. And Sarine knew he wasn't lying. There were hardly any night clubs in town, and the women who went to them were not the type who could make use of such low-cut creations.

"Well, how much?" Sarine said. "I don't want to bargain with you."

He fingered two or three of the satin dresses.

"Fifty dollars?"

"I need a hundred," she said honestly. "Will you buy them for that? You know what they're really worth."

She saw that she couldn't impress him. He began folding the dresses up and piling them neatly one on top of the other.

"The most I can do for you is seventy-five."

Immediately Sarine unhooked the gold watch on her wrist which she hadn't thought about until this moment. It was a high school graduation present from her father. He had sent it to her from Italy or wherever he had been that particular summer. The watch had been her only real evidence that she had a father at all. She didn't know where he was now. Maybe Japan. Maybe Alaska. Not that it mattered.

"And this?" she said, dropping the watch into his palm.

The man looked at it and sighed a tired sigh. Sarine could tell that he hated buying souvenirs.

He lifted a magnifying glass to his eye and examined the circle of diamonds around the face.

"This is a fine piece," he murmured thoughtfully.

"Well?"

"All right," he said, slipping the watch into his vest pocket. "I'll give you a hundred for everything."

Sarine accepted the money, shut her empty valise and left.

As she strolled back toward her room, she began to feel good about not having to borrow money from Paul. Why, indeed, had she thought of doing that in the first place? Since pawning things was almost habitual with her, she felt no particular pain about the transaction. She could go home now and pack her few clothes and get right out of this town.

But the money in her purse made her anxious. If she didn't get the plane ticket right away, she might very well spend too much of it on food or clothes or something. The smartest thing she could do would be to get to the ticket agency right away.

So she turned the corner and headed for the tiny shopping center of the town.

A young girl with blonde hair that dipped softly over her forehead hung up the phone and came over to Sarine. Photographs of airplanes and scenes from foreign countries hung about the room, lending their blue to the blue of the girl's eyes.

"May I help you?"

"Yes, please." Sarine stood the valise beside her and started to take out the money.

"I'd like a tourist flight to New York. This evening, if possible."

How delicious to get away from here without any fuss. No goodbyes, no promises to write.

The girl consulted a chart on the desk beside the telephone. "There's a flight out at seven-twenty," she said. "The limousine will take passengers out to the airport at ten to seven. It stops at First and Main Streets." She spoke as though the speech were memorized.

"That'll be fine." Sarine counted out seventy-eight fifty, then tucked a small wad of singles and a couple of tens back into her bag.

Calmly she waited while the girl wrote out the ticket and spoke about unimportant details that Sarine barely heard. What did she care if there were a half hour stop in Chicago?

With the act of putting the ticket into her purse, Sarine felt breathlessly close to New York. In a little over an hour, she would be on her way at last.

Sarine hurried back to her rooming house. And before she opened the door, she knew that someone was in her room.

She could feel a lingering, angry presence, as one senses an oncoming disaster. Though the door was shut tight, she felt someone waiting for her on the other side.

Turning the knob with a quick gesture, she flung the door open.

"Hi," Cozy said.

He wasn't drunk now. In fact he was terribly sober. He lounged in her chair, his legs in neatly pressed trousers comfortably crossed in front of him. He puffed casually on a new cigar.

It struck Sarine as rather strange that Cozy had been able to pull himself together so quickly. She wasn't sure that she liked the superficial good will of his pleasant manner. And it angered her that he had so blithely made himself at home.

But she couldn't linger out in the hall. She stepped inside and closed the door.

"Glad to see you looking better," she said and hoped that their conversation would continue smoothly until one of them left. She wondered if Cozy knew about the plane ticket. He wasn't above having her followed. Maybe Anna was continuing her duties as a spy for him.

"Forget about this afternoon," he said with a self-conscious laugh. "A guy has his ups and downs."

"Don't we all."

She put down the suitcase and noticed Cozy looking at it. She didn't want to pack while he was here. It seemed that every step of her way was littered with Cozy's mud puddles.

"Buy yourself a new travelling case?" he said.

She knew that he knew it was the same worn valise that she had carried when she first came to town.

"Yeah," she said. "I found a bargain." If he wanted to play cat and mouse, maybe it would be wiser to go along with him. If he only knew how sick to death she was of his face.

"You'll never believe it," he said, "but I've been doing a lot of thinking."

Oh, she believed it all right. He'd probably worked out a field marshal's strategy to get in her way. Sarine got herself a glass of water from the sink and sat down on a hassock. She tried not to let Cozy see her impatience with him.

"What I've been thinking," he continued, "is that there're going to be a lot of changes around the Jingo Club. First of all, I think we should start advertising. How would you like to see yourself spread all over the Sunday section of the *Record*?" Beneath his air of pretended self-satisfaction, he was watching her anxiously. So he had come here to test her, to see if she would forget this afternoon and return to the happy paradise of Cozy's arms—and the Jingo Club.

"I thought you were broke," she said flatly.

"Oh, well," he stared hard at the ash on his cigar. "Broke one day, millionaire the next. You know how it goes in show business."

His tone suddenly revolted Sarine.

"Look, Cozy," she said. "I've got a few things to do that require privacy. If you don't mind, I wish you would leave."

He didn't make any move to get up. One would have thought she had no right to a will of her own.

"You didn't hear anything," he said. "All the plans."

"I'm not interested." She put down the glass and stood up. "I'm not interested in anything that has to do with the Jingo Club except the money you owe me."

"Oh, that," he waved the cigar. "You know I'm good for it. When have I ever tried to cheat you out of anything? Why, that would be like stealing food from my left hand. Now, why don't you sit down and listen to all the things that I want to organize?"

"Because I don't want to sit down. I wish you'd go."

She could see him struggling not to lose his patience. He licked at his mustache and tried to preserve the smile.

"You can't be in all that much of a hurry," he said. "No shows to do tonight. Nothing."

"That's my business. Now, I don't want to have to ask you again."

He put up his hands defensively. "All right. I'll go. But we're still friends, aren't we?"

Sarine shrugged. "Why not?"

"Then as a friend, maybe you could give me some advice. You know I never make a move without asking you about it first."

"What kind of advice do you want?" she said, glancing at the clock. It was ten after six.

"Well, first of all, about a band. Do you think it would be worth having a feature band with the feature singer?"

She could tell he was stalling.

"I don't know anything about publicity," she said. "Maybe we could talk about it some other time."

"Come on. You're not going anyplace, Sarine. What say we have a little drink together and talk this thing out over dinner? If a man wants to bury the hatchet, you'd think his girl would give him the chance."

"Once and for all—"

"No, don't interrupt me." He came over to her and put his hands on her shoulders.

The stench of his cigar seemed more repulsive now than ever.

"I admit I've been a little foolish in the past couple of days," he said. "But that's what makes me human. A woman should be glad when her man gets jealous. I knew you were only giving me a hard time about Paul. Even when I got angry, I knew deep down that there couldn't ever really be anything between you and that shnook. Besides, what could he do for you? Would he work himself to the bone trying to figure a way to make a star out of you? Why, he doesn't even earn enough money to get himself a decent suit."

"Cozy, if you don't take your hands off me and get out of here this instant, I'm going to scream."

And out of sheer exasperation, Sarine felt as though she would.

"What is it with you, anyway? You so set on New York?"

"Cozy, I—"

"I'll take you to New York if that's all you want. Think it's such a big deal to go there? Why, we could leave tomorrow and spend as long as you'd like. No point in getting upset over a little thing like that."

Sarine could see the bluff shining clear and bright in his eyes. But even if she wanted to, she didn't have time to humor him. She had to pack and make herself look decent.

She pulled herself away from his grip and swung the suitcase on the bed.

"What are you doing?"

"Packing, Cozy. Just what it looks like."

He grunted in confusion.

"But I thought we were going out this evening."

He didn't try to stop her. He merely stood and watched her transferring things from the drawers into the suitcase.

She didn't answer him. She had really nothing more to say. If he wanted to hang on until the bitter end, that was his own concern.

"When are you going?"

"Tonight."

He waited for a few seconds, as though gathering up steam.

"I suppose you thought this all through very carefully. You know there's a job waiting for you when you get to New York."

Sarine realized that not answering him was a good policy. He would keep right on talking, even if it were to himself. At least there would be no arguments that way. Let him vent all his sarcasm, all his anger. She could close her ears to it and think about New York.

"Well," he said. "I don't hear you answering me. Could it be that you don't have a job waiting for you? Maybe you're going to New York on a bet and you're ashamed to admit it to me. Can that be what it is, Sarine? Can it?" He came over and put his hand on the suitcase.

She let him stand there and watch her every move. Beneath her outward calm she felt herself boiling with fury.

"No answer, huh? So I'm right." He let his hand slide down on her folded blouses.

"You're in my way," she said, not looking at him.

"You're not answering me." He toyed with a pair of folded stockings and slowly lifted them out of the valise. "We're friends. You don't have to bluff me, Sarine. I admit my mistakes. Why don't you admit yours?"

As she saw him begin to lift out the top blouse, Sarine felt her patience snap.

"Get out. Go on, get out."

She pushed him away from the valise. He caught her wrist.

"You're not going anywhere." He caught her other arm and held them tightly together.

She tried to kick him and he pushed her on the bed.

"I said you're not going anywhere."

Before she could stop him, he dumped the valise upside down and began ripping her underwear.

She saw the burning color in his cheeks. His eyes, large with fury, seemed to smile with an almost insane delight. Sarine knew she couldn't stop him. As she watched him destroy her clothes, she became suddenly detached from her own anger. Surreptitiously she edged toward her purse. She must reach that purse and get out of here.

Consumed by his need for violence, Cozy did not notice her. She grasped the purse. With a quick, determined movement, she propelled herself off the bed and out of the room. She raced down the hall and reached the safety of the street. As she went hurriedly along the block, Sarine looked around for a taxi, hoping to find one and escape before Cozy could catch up with her.

As she slammed the cab door and directed the driver to go directly to the airport, Sarine heard Cozy's voice calling after her. She rolled up the window and settled back. The cab sped toward the outskirts of town.

When the lights of the airport came into view, Sarine felt so grateful that she was glad to count out the last of her extra dollars, just for the relief of being away from Cozy at last. He wouldn't dare follow her out here. She was through with him, and finished forever with everyone like him.

Sarine walked into the ladies' room, fixed her hair and straightened out her clothing. She had no luggage to declare and only a twenty-five dollar reserve.

She came out of the lounge and traversed the waiting room to stand where she could see the runway. The smell of gasoline filled the evening breeze. Now she heard the powerful roar of a six-engined plane as it came in for a landing. In a little while she would step aboard such a plane. And tomorrow meant New York, Jerry Lutha, and the fulfillment of all her dreams.

CHAPTER SIX

SARINE BOARDED THE plane, waited anxiously until she was safely aloft beyond Cozy's reach, and then promptly fell asleep. The drone of the motors did not disturb her, nor did the chattering of two youngsters in the seat behind. Nothing could touch Sarine now. With each passing moment, her problems lay further away. Her heavy slumber was not even burdened with dreams.

Somewhere around two in the morning, Sarine awoke and accepted a container of coffee from the stewardess. Thoughtfully she sipped at the hot liquid and realized that Paul was flitting through her mind. He seemed to be the only broken link in her chain of plans.

Beside her an old lady snored fitfully. Sarine turned away to stare out at the blackness beyond the window. What if Paul had gotten into some kind of trouble? If Cozy really believed that Paul had caused the rift between himself and Sarine, he would be capable of violence. The possibility of this disturbed Sarine more than she wished to admit. Surely Paul could take care of himself in a fight. But if Cozy were seeking revenge, he would hardly challenge Paul on a man-to-man basis.

She beckoned to the stewardess and asked for pen and paper. After much consideration she wrote a brief letter to Paul, requesting that he get in touch with her through Jerry Lutha. Feelings of pride made writing the note difficult but her concern for Paul was more important than her pride. She addressed the letter to Paul in care of the musicians' union. Of course, there was the great possibility that he would not receive it, but she had to make this gesture.

When she had sealed the letter and placed it in her purse, Sarine stretched her legs and tried to fall asleep again. The quiet atmosphere of resting passengers soothed her until wakefulness subsided.

She awoke for the second time at the Chicago stopover. Sleepily she stepped out of the plane. A fierce wind snapped her fully awake. Shivering, she hurried into the waiting room. Watching the other passengers put on overcoats, she realized her own lack of foresight. The old lady from the plane waddled over to her and said,

"Dearie, you're going to catch your death."

Sarine mustered a smile. "I'll be all right, thank you."

"No, you won't. Better take this." She unzipped a battered travelling bag and pulled out a long hand-knit shawl.

"Really, I don't—"

"Nonsense."

Before Sarine could stop her, the woman put the shawl around her shoulders and draped the ends into the crooks of her arms. Despite her protestations, Sarine felt grateful for the protecting warmth. The rough wool hugged her shoulders comfortingly.

"And don't take it off until we're back aboard the plane. Your mother should know better than to let you go away practically naked."

Blushing under her tan, Sarine thanked the woman once more and offered to watch her bag while the woman went to the ladies' lounge.

She stood gazing after the squat figure as it disappeared between the swinging doors. Sarine laughed to herself, but she began to wonder if she really looked so young and helpless. The idea of not being able to take care of herself was, naturally, completely nonsensical. No one had ever really taken care of Sarine—she had never given any one the chance. Fingering the shawl, she considered what it must be like to relax and let someone else take over the responsibility.

When they reboarded the plane, the old woman became talkative. Fortunately she didn't ask Sarine questions about herself but merely described her own life and trials throughout the years. Sarine felt rather glad for the company of this harmless person. Not often did she have the time or the inclination to listen to things that didn't relate to show business. The idea of diapers or sitting up nights with a child who had measles was as strange an idea to Sarine as traveling to Mars.

In a short while, the stewardess came to tell them to fasten their seat belts.

Excitedly Sarine looked out the window and saw the flashing lights of Idlewild shining in the oncoming dawn. She saw the haze of buildings packed tightly together. New York, with all its glamor, its competition, its hurrying drive toward success seemed to lie at Sarine's feet. A desire to conquer surged through her. The voice of the old lady became dim to her ears.

With impatience she watched as the plane slid down on the runway. Patches of gold and red peeked over the horizon as though swept raggedly by the swift winds.

She watched the debarking steps being wheeled toward the plane. Forcing herself to act with decorum, Sarine waited her turn to step out onto the wonderful earth of New York.

Only after she reached the lobby did Sarine's good spirits begin to flounder. Now that she had arrived, where was she going? A cheap hotel, of course. But do you just tell the cab driver to take you to a cheap hotel? She had had her fill of them. Full well did she know what a girl had to contend with in a slum hotel.

She tilted her chin up and told herself, so what? This was part of the game. She could put up with whatever came her way. Besides, she could go see Jerry Lutha that very afternoon. If she were lucky, he should have gotten back to the city last night. Surely he would find suitable living quarters for her.

A line of cabs waited at the exit and Sarine got into the first one.

"Look, mister," she said. "Can you take me to a reasonable hotel in Manhattan?"

"Sure. Which one?" He took the wrapping off a stick of gum, rolled it into a ball and flicked it out the window.

"Any one. I don't care."

He chewed the gum and looked at her slowly. "New in town, eh?"

"Yes."

"Planning to be a big star on Broadway?" he said. "So the folks can read about it in the hometown paper?"

Sarine crossed her legs and realized she was still wearing the old lady's shawl. It made her look like a hick.

"What about the hotel?" she said.

"Pardon me for breathing," he answered, shifted the cab into gear and swung off toward the highway.

She knew she'd better not snub the driver. If he wanted to get even with her, if he thought she was a snob, Sarine was at his mercy.

"I'm just in from the coast," Sarine offered. "And tired to death."

He looked at her in the rear view mirror.

"Yeah, I can see that," he said in a somewhat softened tone.

Sarine felt a little reassured. The heater sent warm air back toward her and she rolled up the window so that none of it would escape. Not only was she tired, but her body ached from the unaccustomed cold. She looked out at the trees standing bleak and bare of leaves. The atmosphere had a withered and depressing tone and all the houses along the road looked shut up to battle away the weather.

Her summer dress and open shoes would not be adequate. She must look like a freak, a nut blown in from some Horseville. Sarine yearned for a hundred dollars and a map of the department stores.

The clicking meter raced upward as the car sped along. She didn't dare consider what would happen if she didn't have enough money to pay the fare.

Soon the dirt smell of the city came to her nostrils and Sarine looked about her at the buildings smeared black and the narrow streets beginning to crowd with early morning traffic.

"I'm taking you to a pretty nice joint in midtown," the driver said. "You'll make out okay."

She heard the meaning behind the words. Perhaps he didn't know that she understood what he was implying. Or perhaps it was his way of offering to take out the cab fare in trade. Well, she wasn't that far gone yet. In just a couple of hours, she'd have plenty of cash to keep her going. No prospect of having to put out faced her. Of course, if it became necessary in the course of events, that would be okay. But right now she preferred to believe that everything in her future depended on her musical talent rather than on the hidden talents of her body. Or were they so hidden? She tugged the hem of her skirt discreetly below her knees.

As the cab made its way uptown, Sarine absorbed everything she could see. Greedily her gaze took in this wonderful and weird city that could rocket you to heaven or drag you down to nightmarish depths.

"Okay, lady," the driver said as he shut off the meter. "You ain't got no baggage so the desk clerk might give you a hard time. But stick to your guns. He knows we all have to earn a living."

Purposely Sarine ignored the last slur. She took out one of her last tens and told him to keep the change.

Then she hurried through the wind and up the steps and came into a lobby that presented worn sofas and a pale tan décor. Except for a thin desk clerk, the room was empty. The smell of old cigarette smoke mixed with a faint odor of garlic. But she paid no attention to these things, hoping only that she had enough cash to last until she found Jerry Lutha.

“Morning,” the desk clerk smiled at her from behind tortoise shell glasses. His smooth face told Sarine that he couldn’t be much older than herself. Yet there were deep circles beneath his eyes which made him look worried, uneasy and even old.

“I’d like a single room, please.”

He studied her tan.

“For how long?”

“A couple of nights, I suppose. Depending.”

His mouth opened as though to comment but he said nothing. Instead he asked, “With or without bath?”

Oh, how she would have loved to take a bath. “Without, if you have it.”

He glanced over the wall of mail compartments and lifted off a key. “The porter’ll help you with your bags,” he said in a voice that knew very well she didn’t have any.

“That won’t be necessary,” Sarine said bluntly.

He smiled at her with the kind of smirk very familiar to Sarine. She smiled back with the bland cold smile that had shattered older and more experienced men than this punk.

“That’ll be two-fifty a night, unless you want it by the week,” he said.

“No. I’ll take it for the night.”

“Very well.” He handed her a pen and she scribbled her name on the register. It comforted Sarine to know that someday this kid might be wanting her autograph.

To her surprise, he didn’t ask for payment in advance but signalled for the bell hop. She put down a five dollar bill anyway, which he folded and slipped into his pocket.

The bell boy took her upstairs in a squeaking elevator and opened the door of her room. She thanked him, gave him half a dollar and closed the door behind him.

Sarine dropped her purse on the bed and looked out the window to a brick wall. The heavy musty smell made breathing unpleasant and she flung the window open, glad for the rush of cold air though it made her shiver.

Absently she looked at her watch and realized that her wrist was bare. How many times she had looked without consciousness of the time piece. Now that it was gone, she became aware of all the years it had been present.

New York, she told herself again. I've finally made it. Then she sat down on the faded green bedspread and lay her head back on the lumpy pillows. Staring up at the porcelain chandelier, she wondered how long since anyone had wiped off the dust. The whole ceiling was covered with a layer of gray filth in which she could have written her name. Beneath her body, the mattress poked at her spine. She needed to stretch out like this but the bed did not seem to offer rest.

The silence was suddenly shattered by a radio blaring from the room across the hall. She looked around and saw that there was an old brown radio on the night table beside the bed. A metal plate fixed to its side told Sarine that for a quarter she could have fifteen minutes of undisturbed listening.

Suddenly she remembered her dress. Bouncing up from the bed, she considered herself in the dressing table mirror and examined all the wrinkles which told of her trip. She couldn't go to see Jerry Lutha like this. She slipped out of her clothes and phoned room service.

The desk clerk's voice said, "May I help you?"

Quite politely she asked if it were possible to have her things pressed.

Then she cradled the receiver and waited for someone to come get her clothes. How could she let a man into the room when she didn't even have a bathrobe? The slip she wore covered her breasts adequately, but you could see beneath it to the outline of her bra and panties. If a man came in and saw her in this state of undress, how could he help but think that she was looking for trouble? Or business, as the cab driver said. But she had to have it done, better to fight a man off than appear so unkempt before Jerry Lutha. Maybe she could open the door just wide enough to put the dress through without the man seeing her. Unhappily she waited for the knock.

When she heard knuckles tap lightly on the door, Sarine said, "Just a minute." Then she opened the door an inch and shoved the dress outward.

When she had closed the door again, a voice on the other side said, "If you'll just let me in a minute—I have to give you a receipt."

"Slip it underneath the door," she said.

"I'm sorry, miss, but it won't go."

She knew that wasn't the truth. She hadn't even heard him try.

"All right." Again she opened the door just an inch. "You'll have to hand it to me this way," she said. "I'm sorry, but I'm not dressed."

A grumble of annoyance came in response and a couple of fingers pushed a piece of cardboard through the opening.

"When can I expect it?"

"About seven or so."

"But I only want it pressed." How could she sit up in this room alone and practically naked for all those hours?

"I'll try to get it done sooner for you, but don't count on it."

Sarine heard his footsteps retreat down the hall. She threw the door open and put her head out.

"Wait a minute," she called, not caring about her state of undress. "Come back."

The man turned and came grumbling back.

"I'll have to get this done somewhere else," she said, taking the dress off his arm.

"Have it your own way." He stared at the flesh swelling out over her brassiere.

Quickly she shut the door again and threw the dress on the bed. Her flesh felt sticky with a film of dirt and the cold air made her limbs stiff and unmanageable. She supposed that there must be a place in the neighborhood where she could wait in the dressing room while her dress was being pressed. She would have to go find such an establishment. With distaste she donned her clothing and went out in search.

Ignoring the desk clerk, she stepped out onto the street and hugged the shawl tightly to her. The November wind tore ruthlessly through the thin material of her clothes. Her skin began to burn with the cold. Instinctively she walked close to the sides of the buildings in an effort to shield herself. Weakly a morning sun glimmered from behind a haze of cloud. She had never before seen so pale a sun. The disc shed neither warmth nor cheer, as though it were a pasted up cheap replica of the glowing mass of fire she had known out West.

Sarine made her way up the street, looking for a cleaner's. She found only rows of cheap tie stores, cigar stores and spaghetti joints. Seasoned New Yorkers rushed past with chins half hidden by coat collars and hands jammed stiffly into pockets. The pervading odor of soot mixed with gasoline in the air only helped to make Sarine more uncomfortable.

At last she stopped in a doughnut shop and ordered a cup of coffee. She hardly remembered the last time she had eaten a decent meal, but she wasn't hungry now. When the countergirl put the heavy mug before her, Sarine asked where she might have her dress attended to.

"Three blocks west of here is a place. You just follow the street straight down."

Sarine thanked the girl and finished her coffee, not at all eager to return to the cold.

Finally she paid her check and went in search of the place. Totally ignorant of the neighborhood, Sarine pursued her way into the increasingly rougher streets. She had seen many drunks in her lifetime and they didn't bother her. Paying no attention to the characters in dirty clothes who called out obscene offers as she passed, Sarine kept her gaze intently ahead. Servicemen from all countries, more alone than herself, looked after her body with craving. A policeman clapped his hands together against the cold and inspected her with steely eyes.

The tiny store was nearly hidden, jammed between a pawn shop and a uniform renting establishment.

She stepped quickly inside and felt a rush of steam overwhelm her frozen body. A tall and muscular fellow left the pressing machine that he was working and came over to her.

"Can you press this dress for me right away?"

"Sure," he said, scratching at some sweat in the crook of his arm. "Why don't you take it off and I'll be glad to."

She looked around for a booth but found none.

"Where can I?"

He shrugged. "You're welcome to stand behind that row of suits there, if you're bashful."

Sarine wondered if every man in the entire city was hard up. They seemed like pigeons with feathers forever puffed, circling around and forever looking at her. For spite, she threw the dress over the top of the rack.

"You find it?" she said.

"No," he said and she knew he was lying.

She heard his footsteps coming around to her.

"Where'd you put it?" he said with pretended innocence as his gaze roamed slowly over the curve of her hips.

"I tossed it over," she said angrily.

"Oh."

He made no attempt to move.

"If you don't mind, I'm in a hurry." She moved the shawl to cover her breasts, grateful for its tremendous proportions.

Because she was completely covered now, the man turned around and went to retrieve her garment.

Sarine waited, listening to the steam puff out of the machine. In a few minutes, he brought the dress back on a metal hanger and tried to see beneath the shawl as she reached out.

But Sarine could handle herself very well and she made it evident to this man that he wasn't going to get anything except a cash payment for his job.

"Well, go on," she said.

He ambled away and Sarine slipped quickly into her dress.

When she came back to the street, a barber shop clock told her it was barely ten o'clock. She doubted that Jerry Lutha would be in his office this early, but perhaps she should wait for him there anyhow. The office would undoubtedly be warm and no one would bother her—except possibly that secretary, Mrs. Reinhart.

Sarine found a drug store and looked up Jerry Lutha's business address in a phone book. Good sense told her not to take another cab. But she didn't know her way around the city. And anyway Jerry would take care of her once she reached him.

Happier now with the prospect before her of seeing Jerry Lutha so soon, she combed her hair in front of the drug store mirror and freshened her lipstick. Observing herself objectively, she knew she didn't look so well. The strain of her trip showed in a kind of sloppiness about her face. She needed to lather her skin and pencil her eyebrows. Since there was no help for this, she found another taxi and put the thought out of her mind.

As the cab drove to her destination, she half understood why Paul hadn't relished New York. There was so much of the seamy side. You could go for miles, it seemed, without seeing anything but dejection and poverty. Perhaps the natives knew how to get around without much cash, but an outsider was certainly lost unless he had the money to pay his way.

Just as she was thinking this, the driver turned onto a wide street that looked spacious and clean in contrast to those she had already seen. Looking out the window, she saw a street sign that said Park Avenue. By the numbers on the buildings she knew that

Jerry's office was just a few blocks away. A thrill of excitement scattered the grimness which had dogged her since yesterday and she dusted off the tips of her shoes with her handkerchief.

She entered the building through a large revolving door of brass and sought Jerry Lutha's name on the wall directory. The elevator took her up to the seventeenth floor and she entered Jerry Lutha's office with a tremendous smile warming her from head to toe.

Mrs. Reinhart looked up and recognized Sarine immediately. Her lips came together in a tight expression of disgust. Sarine didn't mind her now. She was so glad to see a familiar face, even this one. She removed the shawl and folded it into a small mass.

"Is Mr. Lutha expecting you?" the woman said.

"No," Sarine replied honestly. "But I'll wait for him if he's busy."

"Well, he isn't here."

"I can wait."

"He won't be in until after lunch."

"That's all right."

The room had half a dozen chairs of black leather arranged neatly against the light blue wall. One small plant sat on the edge of Mrs. Reinhart's desk. Other than this, there was little in the way of decoration to make a stranger feel at home. Clearly this was an office designed for work.

Sarine placed herself in a corner chair and engrossed herself in the sepia photographs of movie and stage stars which lined the walls. A surge of ambition twinged in her. Just knowing what Jerry Lutha had done for others filled her with joy. The possibilities for herself lay unlimited in the future. Gone were her recollections of the dingy hotel, and the episode with her dress fled with all other thoughts of her past struggle.

Mrs. Reinhart rattled the papers in her file as though to tell Sarine there were more important things in this world than to be a proper hostess. Sarine nodded at the woman and smiled cordially. She didn't much care whether Mrs. Reinhart liked her or not, but she had no reason to be uncivil to the woman.

Hardly an hour went by before Jerry Lutha came in. He wore a gray flannel suit with a light blue tie which, like his office, seemed to indicate complete attention to business at hand.

"Good morning, Mr. Lutha," Sarine said. She was not at all surprised that he didn't wear a coat. She felt that the man moved so fast he didn't need anything other than his own steam to keep him warm.

"Well, what the—" He looked at her and frowned. "Come on inside," he said.

Sarine felt grateful that he didn't bawl her out in front of Mrs. Reinhart.

She entered his office and stood looking out over the rooftops from a window that faced south. Dimly she could make out the spire of the Empire State building. Strangely it looked like all the photographs. Sarine had expected New York to be very different from the corny pictures she'd seen.

"Will you please tell me what on earth possessed you?" Jerry Lutha said, not bothering to hide his annoyance.

His anger made her feel very much at home. Only people who knew each other for years acted with this display of honesty.

He unbuttoned his jacket and sat down in the huge swivel chair of the same black leather as the others. But he didn't push it backward and put his feet up on the desk. Instead he put his elbows on the desk and stared hard at her.

Sarine turned away from the window and looked back at the lean pointed face. She remembered how his lips had softened beneath the touch of her own. But she did not possess him. She wondered if anyone could possess him.

"You make it sound disastrous," she said softly.

"Oh, hell." He took a cigarette and looked through the desk for a lighter that worked. "Will you get it out of your head that

I'm a magician? Just because you're here does not mean that I've got a job waiting for you."

"I didn't say you had."

"Then what do you want from me?"

She came over and sat down on the edge of the desk. She knew exactly what she wanted from him and had no doubts that he would supply it if he could.

"Two things."

"God save me," he groaned.

"A loan of five hundred dollars and a decent place to sleep." Her voice did not imply anything intimate. She knew that the best way to approach Jerry was with forthrightness and simplicity.

"You know," he said, "I should stop being amazed at the childishness of my stable of talents. But what person, who is at all sane, comes to this city broke and without know-how?"

The question required no answer. Yet Sarine felt an answer. "There's one thing you've overlooked."

"What's that?"

"Yourself, Jerry Lutha. You are the know-how. Do you think I would have come directly to your office if I didn't trust you to help me out?"

"I tell you, you're talking out of ignorance."

But Sarine never felt more confident. She didn't blame him for not wanting to fork over cash to every new personality he took on. And she certainly wouldn't have intruded herself upon him if it had been possible for her to manage any other way.

"Let's not get involved," Sarine said mildly. "The fact is that I'm here. I need a place to stay and I need some money coming in very soon. Will you help me?"

He scowled past her shoulder, then his face broke out into a wry smile. That delightful gleam in his blue eyes returned to make his face young and strong again.

"Have I a choice?"

Sarine waited at the door while Jerry told Mrs. Reinhart that he would be out for the rest of the day. Sarine didn't smile triumphantly at the woman. She merely wondered how long it would take before Mrs. R. decided to hate her completely.

Jerry took her elbow and led her around the block to where his car was parked. It was a little foreign two-seater that wound its way easily through traffic. He took her to a small but comfortable hotel and paid a month's rent in advance for two rooms and a kitchen.

"It'll be cheaper if you eat home once in awhile," he said dourly.

Sarine laughed and accepted the admonition with pleasure.

Then he took her to a Fifth Avenue department store and purchased a plentiful supply of street clothes, shoes, two evening gowns and a heavy coat. Sarine had all the things sent back to the hotel but wrapped herself into the coat, happy in its protective warmth.

"You know," he said, "I wouldn't do this if I didn't think it was a good investment."

Sarine didn't take this remark as an insult. She fully expected to repay him. She wanted to. Her relationship with Jerry Lutha was to be strictly honest on every level.

"I guess you're about ready for lunch," he said when they had completed all the necessary purchases.

"You're so right."

She felt hungry now. The security of having Jerry Lutha gave her an appetite.

He escorted her to a crowded restaurant where Sarine recognized the faces of many celebrities in the entertainment world. Hardly a minute would pass without someone calling over a greeting to Jerry. She had the feeling that these greetings included her too, although she did not know these people personally. Something about their attitude took for granted that Sarine was in show business too and consequently no outsider.

As a result of this an idea began to grow in Sarine's mind but she didn't tell it to Jerry right away. She wanted to speak with him about it when they were alone. And so she waited until he drove her back to the hotel.

He opened the car door for her then started to get back inside.

"Please," she said. "Will you come upstairs with me for a few minutes?"

"Now what?"

Sarine hadn't implied anything sexual nor did Jerry interpret her request in this way.

With resignation he locked the car and followed her inside. When they reached her rooms, Jerry said, "I want you to understand one thing. Today is the last time you get my undivided attention. Do me a favor and remember that I'm obligated to a lot of other kids."

He didn't have to finish the speech. Sarine knew she had infringed upon her claims to his services. A blush made her avert her gaze from his stern look.

"Okay," he snapped. "What is it?"

Sarine could tell that he was sorry for having scolded her. Beneath the businessman's exterior was much compassion and understanding. Because his own success had not arrived overnight, he respected the battles other people fought to achieve theirs. Perhaps this accounted just as much for his popularity as the side of him which got things done.

Without asking him to sit down, Sarine flopped down on the sofa and took off her shoes.

"I'd like you to take me on a tour of the nightclubs," she said.

"This minute?" he said. "In your bare feet, I suppose."

He sat himself on the arm of the sofa and lighted one of the dozens of cigarettes he consumed daily. The hunch of his posture told Sarine that he must be every inch fatigued. To realize that Jerry Lutha needed sleep as much as any other human being was a strange thought. Childishly she had taken advantage of him by throwing herself on his mercy. Not only was it a lousy thing to do, but she realized that if she continued, she would lose both his respect for her and his interest.

"If you give me a chance to meet the club owners, isn't there a chance that one of them might take to me, as they say? Maybe give me a job for personal reasons?"

Jerry didn't even turn around to talk to her. He sent smoke sailing toward the olive green wall paper. "You mean sleep your way into an engagement? Not a chance, kid. Remember this is New York. There are thousands of gorgeous broads. A guy who's smart enough to own a club is usually smart enough to separate business from monkey business."

"Are you sure?"

She watched the ash of his cigarette fall unnoticed to the rug. "No."

She leaned back in an effort to see the expression on his face. But she could have saved herself the trouble. Now Jerry turned around to face her. His eyes were intently serious and the lids were gray from lack of sleep.

"What you do for fun is none of my business," he said. "But I like to think that the kids working for me have just enough confidence in me not to think it necessary to sell themselves for an engagement."

Sarine hadn't thought of this. In her anxiety to start earning money, she had overlooked Jerry's pride, her own pride, and both their talents. From years of hard experience, she had learned that the entertainment world was hardly the place for morals. But certainly Jerry Lutha was the last man on earth to be naive. She wondered what his real motives were.

"Then what do you suggest?"

"Sit this month out. Get to know the city a little better. I'll introduce you to all the right people, but gradually."

She accepted his words without argument.

"And if you're lonesome," he continued, "I'm sorry but there's precious little you can do about it for the time being."

He smiled at her gently and patted her hand with affection.

Sarine didn't want him to leave. Now that he had brought her aloneness out into the open where she could recognize it, she felt a surging need for human companionship to see her through this first week in a strange and overwhelming city. To no one else could she admit this. Nor would she have faced it herself, if Jerry hadn't been so matter of fact.

"You've been very decent to me," she said. "I don't intend to take advantage of you." Her subdued voice reached out to him in a tacit expression of gratitude.

Sarine noticed that Jerry's fingers still touched her own. Neither of them spoke for awhile and Jerry could have gotten up to leave if he had wanted to. But he remained seated on the arm of the sofa, thoughtfully smoking his cigarette. Sarine began to think that he wasn't as eager to get home as she had imagined.

Reflecting on the day's activities, she decided that Jerry had enjoyed himself despite his protests.

Brashly she said, "Are you married?"

He swung over the arm of the sofa and let himself plop down on the cushions.

"Does it show?" he said. A bitter-sweet grin deepened the laugh lines around his mouth.

"No," she offered. "I just didn't want to infringe upon another woman's time with you."

He mashed out the cigarette and loosened his tie. She saw his body relax deeper into the sofa and knew that he was going to talk about himself.

"Never fear about that. I'm only half married, you see. I separated from Chris about a year ago. She doesn't want to give me a divorce and she doesn't want to give it another try either." His voice sounded now as lonely as Sarine's.

"I guess she's afraid I won't keep up with the alimony checks."

The high whining sound of an ambulance underscored his words.

"It's not easy for people like us to have a successful marriage, is it?" he said. "We're so damned selfish and driving."

For an instant Sarine thought that maybe he was giving her the routine line. But then she admonished herself for being ridiculous. Jerry wasn't the kind of man who appealed to women by acting like a little boy lost. He was revealing himself to her because she had been so honest with him.

"That's why I was so annoyed with you wanting to drag along your piano player." He crossed his legs at the ankles and clasped his hands behind his head. She liked his habit of not looking at her when he talked. He assumed that she was interested in what he had to say; no need to hold her attention with his eyes.

"Let's forget about Paul," she said. "I closed that book days ago."

"Really?" He didn't sound as though he believed her.

Sarine stretched out on the couch and put her head in his lap. Lying on the overstuffed softness of the cushions, she felt her own body begin to ease. The tenseness which had made her spine ache all day began to subside.

"Why don't you believe me?" she said. "Paul and I were friends for awhile, that's all. Oh, he would have liked it to develop into something more, but it never could."

"You told him there wasn't a chance?" He stroked the strands of hair along her temple. "You did the right thing," he said. "I hope you don't regret it now."

Regret it? Paul would only be in her way here, probably trail after her and keep insisting that her true destiny was to be a respectable housewife. Complete foolishness.

"My wife is very much like Paul. Quiet, sensible, clean-living. We struggled along for seven years trying to compromise. It just doesn't work, you know. One or the other has to give in completely or no soap."

Sarine knew he was right and she felt sad for Jerry. Luckily she herself had avoided that pitfall; and now, with him, she was safe from falling into a well-meant trap. She would never allow love to ruin herself or the man who might become involved with her.

Jerry's fingers wandered absently along the side of her cheek. She knew he was thinking of his wife and she didn't feel that as an insult to her own femininity. In fact she would be disappointed if Jerry seemed to be falling in love with her.

She brought his fingers to her lips and kissed them gently. There was no need for her to say how glad she was that they were friends. They knew each other intuitively. Their mutual bond of ambition gave them a kind of telepathy.

He bent over and kissed the side of her mouth. Her body curved upward toward him. She put her hands behind his neck and held his lips firmly on hers. She didn't have to pretend to be in love with him. Nor did she have to say any of the melodramatic words which usually excited a man's desire.

After a while Sarine got up and made Jerry take off his jacket. She went to the refrigerator to mix a couple of drinks and laughed at the unexpected emptiness. How delightful, she realized, that she already felt so at home here. Although there was no refreshment and she didn't even have a bathrobe hanging in the closet, Sarine felt comfortable and thoroughly at home.

Jerry unbuttoned his shirt and hung it over the back of a chair. She heard him go into the bedroom and pull down the bedspread.

"Come on in," he called.

When she came in, he unbuttoned her dress and hung it on one of the metal hangers swinging in the empty closet. Then he lifted up her slip, folded it neatly and laid it on the lounging chair.

"Take a good hot shower," he said. "And wash off that California suntan."

She stepped into the square bathroom of white tile and turned on the faucets.

"Going to join me?" she called.

"I guess so."

They went into the shower and stood very close in the tingle of hot water. Then he turned her around and lathered her back, rubbing the skin briskly with the thick cloth. She submitted to the energy of his rubbing, enjoying without thought the physical and animal pleasure of his touch.

She wanted to soap him all over too, but he made her get out.

"This is one thing I like to do for myself," he burbled.

She stood on the bathmat watching the droplets of water trickle along the outside of her breasts. The mirror, clouded with steam, presented a shadowy form of herself. But even so she could see the difference between the tan of her limbs and the whiteness of her belly. Soon this tan would fade and she would look like a native New Yorker. The thought pleased her and she poked at the shower curtain to tell Jerry to hurry up.

When he came out, the thin strands of his hair plastered over his forehead, she gave him a towel and lifted her arms so that he could dry her. She liked this kind of attention. And she liked to watch the muscles of his chest flex as he rubbed her skin energetically.

He put the towel around her waist and pulled her to him. The freshly cleansed odor of their bodies mingled damply for a long minute.

Then Jerry switched out the light and they padded in darkness to the bed.

He sat down and brought her on his lap. She felt the mounting tension as his kisses became rougher. Gladly Sarine responded to his urgency. She held him tightly to her, wanting to become one with him, so that she would never have to feel that terrible loneliness which so often crept over her.

Sarine responded to his caresses, giving of herself as she had never before given to any man. She did not put her body at his convenience, but rather offered herself freely and happily. She had nothing to gain by merely being a sexual prop. But she had everything to gain by joining him in the comradeship of their bodies. For once she did not feel as though she were being used, and her calculating mind went gladly to rest, allowing her desire to lead her along with Jerry into a world where neither loneliness nor ambition existed.

In the afterglow of their desire, Sarine lay with her mouth against his ear. She did not dare to wonder how long their relationship could go on like this. There was no use fooling herself that the novelty would not wear off for one or both of them in a short time.

Perhaps this was one reason why men like Paul and women like Jerry's wife tried so hard to change the ones they loved. Perhaps they had a superior wisdom that hated the built-in loneliness which so often sapped people like herself and Jerry.

She snuggled up closer to Jerry and tried to believe that they could go on like this for a long time. As she pulled the sheet up to cover them, he was already fast asleep.

CHAPTER SEVEN

SARINE SAW JERRY only twice during the next ten days. He took her to the Mocha Club and to the Red Crow because Sarine couldn't live without the atmosphere of night clubs from which to draw sustenance. Even though she wasn't in the spot light, just to sit and watch a good entertainer belt out the old standard melodies gave Sarine a new thrust of life. Music was the staff of her existence.

Her enforced idleness didn't help soothe her nerves. Dutifully she visited the Planetarium and the Museum of Modern Art and Radio City. She didn't mind going alone except that these activities made her feel as though she were marking time. When she returned to her hotel each evening, her mind would scurry along avenues of thought in the hope of finding some outlet for her restlessness.

One morning as she was opening a box of pancake mix the idea came to her. She left the utensils askew in the kitchen and hurried to get dressed.

Then she hailed a cab and directed the driver to take her to one of the recording studios that Jerry had pointed out to her. She ran up the narrow flight of stairs, paid the attendant enough money to have the room for herself all day, and sat down at the piano to practice.

Sarine's fingers moved stiffly over the keys. She knew just enough technique to accompany herself with the basic chords. But these chords were vivid in her mind. She paid little attention to the bare room or the upright that wasn't quite in tune. Her enthusiasm filled in for these defects as she made Paul's music come to life again. As she played she remembered the many times they had gone through these songs together, just in private, for the two of them—these weren't spectacular numbers to appeal to the customers of the Jingo Club. They were substantial lyrics and melodies, timeless in their appeal to the heart.

As she played Sarine realized why Paul would never make out in New York. He and his music had a way of reaching right down to the core of a person and displaying that core without shame, without deviousness. In music this was fine. But in dealing with people who were in a hurry to get ahead, you had to be careful about their private weaknesses. Paul was too honest. And he knew it.

She practiced half a dozen of his songs to smooth out her style, and then made the recordings. Handling the precious discs with care, she called Jerry from a pay phone and told him to wait for her at his office.

Mrs. Reinhart was just putting on her hat as Sarine came in. Sarine nodded a quick greeting and hurried past her.

"What is it now?" Jerry said, swinging his feet off the desk.

Sarine put the records on a chair and started to open the package. "Where's your phono?" she said.

"Press that first brass knob." He pointed at the wall.

Without bothering to remove her coat, Sarine pressed the knob and waited while a door flush with the wall swung open to reveal a recording-phonograph combination.

"Do you think you'd like to catch your breath first?" Jerry said. He took a pint bottle of scotch out of the bottom drawer of his desk. "I'm getting good at hiding these things from Mrs. R.," he winked.

Sarine felt a twinge of disturbance. She pushed aside her dark hair and took off her coat. The purpose of her visit retreated as she began to conjecture about Jerry's drinking. He was the last man on earth she would suspect of being an alcoholic.

"Supposing we wait until later for that." She forced a smile and an air of nonchalance.

Jerry shrugged. "As you wish," he said and took a quick gulp from the bottle.

Sarine shuddered inside herself. For an instant her enthusiasm faltered as honest concern for Jerry swept through her. But she dare not say one word.

She put the first record on the turntable and let it play. Then she sat down in one of the leather chairs and watched his expression. But he refrained from comment until she had played them all. And she could not tell from his face what he thought about them.

"Well?" she said.

"Play that second one again."

Encouraged, Sarine placed the record on the turntable and they listened to it in silence.

"When did you do them?" he said, holding the bottle on his lap.

"Today. That's my playing in the background."

"Poor kid."

"Stop avoiding me, Jerry. What do you think of them?"

He spun the ash tray on his desk, then emptied its contents abruptly into the waste paper basket.

"They're magnificent," he answered flatly. "And you don't have to tell me who wrote them."

"What difference does that make?" she said irritably.

"None. None at all."

"So now what do we do?"

He slipped the bottle back into the drawer and shut it with a loud noise.

Mrs. Reinhart knocked on the door.

"Come in, dear."

She opened the door half a dozen inches and put her nose through the space. "I'll be leaving now, if you're finished for the day."

"Sure. See you in the morning."

Sarine came over and pushed his feet aside so she could perch on the desk.

"Well, what do we do?" she repeated.

"Nothing," he said without emotion. "Absolutely nothing." He took out a comb and ran it through his hair. His hair hadn't fallen out of place and Sarine knew that the gesture was a last one for the day before going home.

"Why?" Her voice was agitated. "For heaven's sake, why nothing?"

"Because," he said simply, you are still an unknown. After you've sung at a club for awhile, we can put these out and stand to make a couple of dollars. It wouldn't be good business to try for publicity when nobody has seen your face or heard your style. Put them in mothballs for another couple of months and then we'll have a look see."

Sarine felt herself deflate. For once she didn't have the desire to argue with him.

"By the way," Jerry said, "are they copyrighted?"

She was certain that Paul hadn't bothered with such formalities. "I don't think so."

"Then I'd advise you to do something about that, first." He stood up and brushed a few pieces of lint from his trousers.

"Like what?"

"Either send some copies in yourself or find Paul to do it."

Find Paul! She had received no answer to her letter. But now things were different; she could write to him again. She had a legitimate reason for needing to get in touch with him.

"Don't look so happy about it," Jerry said dourly. "Took you all this time to find an excuse for getting in touch with him. But you made it. I'm proud of you."

Sarine couldn't believe that Jerry wanted to hurt her. She struggled not to lash back with equally cruel words. But why should he want to accuse her so unjustly? She had done nothing to deserve this.

"What can I do," she asked, "'to convince you that I'm not concerned anymore about Paul?" Her voice was even, her manner forthright. She didn't want to parry his trusts, but to understand their motives.

Jerry went over to put the phonograph back in place. "I'm sorry, kid. But you haven't really gotten him out of your system, you know."

"Nonsense!" And wholeheartedly she did believe that Paul meant nothing particularly important to her. How could he? They hadn't spent enough time together to get involved. And besides, she was married to her career. Jerry of all people should know that.

"Well, regardless of what you think," she continued, managing to steady herself, "what's the best thing to do about his music?"

"Find him, of course," Jerry said. "That's the hell of it."

Sarine explained briefly what had happened between Paul and herself and Jerry promised he would do whatever he could to help find him.

A week and yet another week passed by. Sarine wandered along Fifth Avenue listening to the Christmas carols which blared from the large department stores. She sloshed through the dirtied snow and now and then fed a lone sparrow who darted from the limb of a bleak tree.

No sign of Paul. No word. Nothing. Often she turned Jerry's words over in her mind. She searched within herself to find how much she really missed Paul. But the excitement of life in New York compared with Paul's retiring manner always won. At this point, she was positive Paul meant nothing to her.

At last Sarine's engagement came due and she had time for nothing but rehearsals. Jerry's promise had been worth waiting for. Sarine opened in a plush cocktail room of one of the best hotels.

All morning of the day she was due to open Sarine stalked around her apartment, enjoying the tenseness that filled her with excitement. Jerry stayed with her, grooming her with soft words that she didn't even hear. Nor did she need them. Thank heaven she could feel this thrill. If she were cold or blasé about her debut, it wouldn't come off well at all; the vitality would be missing.

After a light lunch, Sarine managed to take a nap. For an hour she lay sleeping in a peculiar state of alertness. Then she took a cold shower, dressed and went with Jerry to the hotel.

Jerry stood at the door of her dressing room like a watch dog. She didn't want to see anyone or have anyone wish her the usual words of good luck. She didn't need luck. She needed only her own crest of vitality to enliven the songs which she would offer. With deliberate calm and careful attention to costume, Sarine slowly perfected her appearance. Her rose-colored gown honored each curve of her body like a young lover.

At last the moment approached and Sarine stood in readiness. She heard the orchestra play her cue. Jerry winked at her and she winked back, then stepped out on the small circular stage.

A fanfare of polite clapping greeted her. Sarine looked out to the dimly outlined couples who sat expectantly at the tables. Here and there a diamond flashed in the pale candlelight, like fireflies in the dusk. The waiters stood along the wall. No glasses clinked. No chatter disturbed Sarine in the spotlight. Wrist high she lifted one hand in the flame of her spotlight. The heat of the bulb warmed her skin almost to burning. A hint of sweet perfume reached her nostrils.

Then, with all the love she possessed, Sarine began the melody of her song. She sang with all the vibrant passion that lived inside her. The devotion that no man could capture for himself she gave now freely to her audience. The band leader, feeling her every breath, held his orchestra to a subtle background for her throbbing voice. Each note reached out to caress her listeners. Pure as first passion, Sarine gave of herself.

And she felt her audience respond. These sophisticates who had seen and heard everything listened to Sarine as though they had never heard song before. She felt them incline their bodies toward her without realizing that they too were giving of themselves. Sarine made with her audience a pact of beauty and harmony.

When she reached the end of her repertoire, Sarine's devotion rewarded her with flowing applause that called again and again for encores.

When she had bowed her way out of the spotlight, she knew she had accomplished her purpose. Success was hers now, without doubt. She could ask her price and get it. In time her name would be legend with the other greats of music. The worst hurdles had been conquered. A well of joy released itself inside her.

Sarine went back to her dressing room subdued from her complete fulfillment. She collapsed into Jerry's arms and nodded dim thanks to the dozen or so people milling around her.

"You were great," Jerry whispered. "There'll be no stopping you now."

After the second performance that night, she allowed herself to be swept away to the first of many parties that she was to enjoy in honor of her talent.

And in a very short time she paid back the money that Jerry had lent her.

The people for whom she worked were only slightly different from all those she had known throughout her erratic career. The bartenders were just bartenders, and the owner of the hotel had a yen which he did not trouble to disguise. Sarine's greatest pleasure was the audience. No cat calls. No brawling. They sat still with a quiet she had almost mistaken at first for boredom.

"You're a good girl, Sarine," the owner told her one night after closing. He was a very old man who relegated the actual business duties to his three sons. But he wasn't so old that his yellowing eyes didn't appreciate a young female body.

"If I were thirty years younger," he chuckled to himself.

"Thanks, Sam," she said. He wanted her to call him by his first name because it made him feel more intimate with her.

She let Sam take her to parties because he was harmless. The men and women whom she met were all very rich and all very restless. She saw dozens of Cozys in hand-made dinner jackets and listened to them reel off unguarded propositions. No, it wasn't very different from the third rate joints she had known all her life. But plenty of servants made living easier and the growing reserve in her bankbook added perspective to Sarine's view of her career.

Only at three or four in the morning, when she was finally alone in her apartment, did Sarine pause a moment to discover that she hadn't brought her smile home with her. But she soon learned to go directly asleep and let her dreams struggle with the problem of loneliness.

Every so often Sam would drop by in the morning to have breakfast with her. She would let him kiss her or touch her with what was supposed to be fatherly affection. She didn't really care. If Sam got a thrill out of this, she was glad that he could enjoy himself.

Eventually she let Sam and Jerry get her an engagement at one of the larger nightclubs along Broadway. Everybody was being kind to her. She didn't save the newspaper clippings but she did read them with satisfaction. The name of Sarine Duvalle was beginning to make a dent. Occasionally strangers pointed her out to each other when she walked along the street. A part of her felt ecstatic about her success. Yet another part stubbornly remained unfulfilled. She flung herself into the whirling routine of the nightclub industry. Nobody worked harder than she. Her repertoire grew to include hundreds of song routines. Oldtimers came to hear her sing. She loved to bring a tear to the eyes of rich old men who thought themselves callous beyond redemption.

And Jerry handled her well. She became his star property and they saw a great deal of each other for purposes of mutual profit.

Christmas came and went. And on New Year's Eve Jerry pulled together a shindig and Sarine met the few remaining personalities whom she had not met during the past months. She even drank champagne without thinking about it. Champagne had become more common to her life than coffee. But over the rim of her glass she watched Jerry become slowly drunk. She worked her way through the crowd and came up to his side.

"Hi, chicken," she said and put her arm around him. She realized with a sudden fright that Jerry was leaning against her for support.

"Having fun?" he said and licked his lips so that they shone too wetly.

She smiled and nodded.

He took her hand and squeezed it. "Tell you what," he said. "Let's you and me go into the coat room back there and have a private conversation."

Jerry extricated himself from the circle of blondes and redheads who had been listening to his every word because he was the great Jerry Lutha.

"Good idea," she answered. "We haven't seen each other for so long." They had spent the past week together, but she said it because one of the blondes looked at Jerry with a dirty smirk.

She took his hand and led him to the coat room only to find a couple lying on the bed, heaving and grunting. Sarine shut the door quickly and they went on back through the crowd in the direction of the library. The huge apartment was Jerry's special place for social engagements. He didn't enjoy living in an eight room penthouse any more than Sarine enjoyed her three room hotel suite. For privacy and comfort Jerry rented a small flat down in the Village which few people other than Sarine knew about.

They entered the library and switched on the lights to find another couple very engrossed with each other on the floor. Sarine recognized both the man and the woman and knew that each was married to someone else. She didn't feel disturbed by this. Her primary emotion was a sensation of being fortunate enough not to have gotten herself similarly involved. She was free as she had always wanted to be free. Money, fame, opportunities of all sorts were coming her way and she was able to avail herself of whatever she might desire. She felt glad and proud to have maneuvered so well.

"Come on," Jerry said, "let's settle down someplace already."

"I'm trying," she said.

They wound up in the kitchen at a little table piled with a reserve of martinis. The extra servants who had been hired for the night bustled past them without taking notice.

"Now, I may not be exactly businesslike tonight and this may not be exactly the right atmosphere. But if you promise not to tell anybody till Monday morning, I've got a little surprise for you." He fumbled inside his jacket pocket and took out a long envelope.

She took the papers he handed over and read a contract for the recording of Paul's music. A thrill of real excitement went through her. She had not felt this sincerely happy about anything since her opening night in New York.

"Bet you thought I was going to forget all about it," Jerry said and grinned with self-satisfaction.

Sarine dared not ask the first question that shot through her mind. He must have found Paul. Otherwise, how could he have negotiated a deal like this?

"Now, now," Jerry said. "Take that eager look off your puss. I didn't find Paul. Oh, I tried all right. Maybe he went home to Podunk or someplace because he sure must be buried."

"Then how—"

"Lawyers can fix anything. It's all very up and up. If Paul wants to come collect his royalties, he's welcome to do so. Ads to that effect are going in all the papers. And he'd be a fool to let so much green stuff flutter away. But anyhow," he picked up two martinis and clinked the glasses together, "here's to a grand success, for a change." With a quick gesture, he swallowed first one and then the other. "I hate martinis," he said.

For the rest of the evening Sarine had to make believe that her mind was on the party. She took Jerry back into the mass of people and jabbered with whomever was in the mood to talk to her. She didn't want to be alone with her knowledge of the contract. A peculiar desire to be as far away from it as possible possessed her tonight. She wanted to enjoy herself and her freedom. Yet something hung like an anchor around her neck, dragging her spirits down into suspicious ideas about herself.

Paul—his name, his stooped shoulders that curved over the piano, his fingers which seemed to be made of pure silver when he played music. No, she definitely didn't want to think about him and his differentness from her and from these laughing, drinking people who were supposed to be her friends.

Somewhere in a corner Jerry had become involved with another young hopeful who stood trying to charm him with her artificial laughter. She couldn't see his face but she could make out the back of his head. The brilliant things that went on in that head made her sad. And she recalled the day he had accused her of feelings for Paul unbecoming to a rising young star. Then she had denied those feelings with sincerity. Now, with the contract in her purse and the odd sensations which made her want to flee from ideas of Paul, she wondered if Jerry hadn't been wiser than she knew.

She tried more champagne and hoped it would make her giggle. The night dragged on and Sarine looked about her to see if people were beginning to leave yet. But even Sam was still making an effort to stay awake. The party could go on past morning. She went to the curtains and drew them aside to see if dawn had begun to rise. Sometimes you could count on cigarettes and cigars to smoke people out of a place. The powerful air-conditioner kept the rooms cool and the air breathable. Endless bottles of alcohol were emptied and returned to the kitchen. Messy leftovers of food were quietly swept away so that the party looked like it had just begun. The people seemed to have wound themselves up extra tight for this evening and no one wanted to be the first to leave. On the contrary, little parties of two's and three's continued to pile in.

Despairingly Sarine found a chair near the curtain and crossed her legs in an effort to sit it out as gracefully as she could. Behind the mask of her party smile, Sarine was trying desperately to understand why Paul insisted on hiding even from Jerry. Surely he couldn't object to a business deal which required no effort from him. He wouldn't even have to come to New York in order to collect his money or sign the necessary papers. He'd be a fool to throw all of this away.

She fought to keep away the possibility that Paul might be dead. Even at four o'clock on a New Year's Eve, the idea seemed preposterous. When Sarine thought of Paul, she thought of all the things in the world which were firm, secure and everlasting. Death held no part in this picture. Her morbidity must be the result of too much champagne and too little sleep.

About eight in the morning the party began to break up. Sarine noticed that the sleek hairdos had become bedraggled and the hollow-eyed women were now far from the glamorous creatures of last night. Fragments of gaiety filled the room with a last despairing effort. Even the flowers sagged and had begun to dry up around the edges.

Jerry was nowhere to be found and so Sarine made goodbyes for him. Finally she plied the last couple loose from their corner of intimacy and escorted them out. Sarine returned the woman's wink and promised to tell all the right people that she was launched on another affair so that it would get into the papers and pick up her waning publicity.

Now Sarine went to the window and drew the curtains. Her gaze feasted on the newborn day that rose crisply pink about the roof tops. Somewhere far below many others lay asleep, peacefully appreciating this extra day of holiday. Tomorrow they would be hurrying to get dressed and finish breakfast and then to jam themselves into the rush hour subways.

But Sarine was no part of this. When others went to work, she slept. As others budgeted, she squandered and couldn't even account for where the money went. No children plagued her with wet diapers. She didn't have to read movie magazines to absorb glamour vicariously. She was Glamour. And just at this moment, Glamour didn't feel very lustrous.

"Happy New Year from me to you. Personal."

Sarine turned to where Jerry was leaning against the jamb of the library door. He had his hands in his pockets and a burned-out cigarette hung between his lips.

"You know something," he said. "I don't think we're ever going to sleep again."

"I know how you feel." She picked up an abandoned canapé and dropped it into an emptied whiskey glass.

"Did you eat too much?" Jerry rolled back his cuffs and moved away from his leaning post.

Sarine shook her head. "As a matter of fact, I didn't eat at all," she said.

"Well, I ate too much and I drank too much and today is a very lousy day that should never have happened. Why don't we go to sleep?"

"I'm too tired for sleep."

"Then we'll take a ride around the park." He came over and sat down on a brocade hassock dark with whiskey stains. "You're supposed to remember one thing." He put his elbows on his knees and stared down at the carpet between his feet.

"And what's that?" Sarine asked, coming to sit down on the floor beside him. She rested her head against his thigh and her gaze traveled over the lines of the grand piano. She felt a strong desire to remove a couple of whiskey glasses that stood on the ebony finish, leaving rings on the beautiful instrument.

"New York is being good to you," he said. "But you're not remembering to be grateful."

"How does it show?"

"You've stopped thinking about your career."

"Oh now, Jerry."

"I'm only warning you for my good, not yours. It doesn't make me feel glad to see number one chicken ignoring all her confreres on the night of Auld Lang Syne."

Sarine knew that Jerry was in the depths of being sober. He had managed to stay drunk through the worst of all the noise and ballyhoo. But now he had come back hard into the empty morning.

"Supposing we talk about this later?" she said and put her lips against the knuckles of his hand.

"Pleasure first, business second?" He slid off the hassock and they lay on the carpet in a long embrace.

"We're very rich people." He kissed her throat.

"We're the top of the world." She nibbled his earlobe.

"We're the dreams that people dream." He slid his fingers along her yielding body.

Sarine wanted Jerry to hurt her so that she would think only of what they were doing. Not of tomorrow nor of yesterday. If she could be part of sex and drown herself in her body's passion, then she could be comforted by at least one refuge from the world.

Neither one spoke now, as they played and dallied with each other. At last, on the rough wool carpet, Jerry grabbed her to him and each found a moment's release from personal destiny.

They slept right there on the floor and neither awoke until the following morning. She waited for Jerry to shower and put on fresh clothes. Then he took her back to her hotel where he waited while Sarine pulled herself together. They had an appointment at eleven o'clock at Pops Recordings and it was now a quarter of eleven. Sarine hurried through her bath and finished making up her face in Jerry's car.

The vice president of Pops greeted them with the languid cordiality that told Sarine he must have had a good breakfast. She felt acutely hungry and not at all nervous. Her belief in Paul's music gave her a self-confidence that allowed her to think about pancakes and syrup instead of impressing the red-cheeked man who was cutting off the tip of a cigar with his tiny silver knife.

"Miss Duvalle, this is a pleasure."

She accepted the stereotyped greeting along with the accompanying handshake and calculated the amount of money he believed she would make for him by the size of his smile.

Sarine watched him pocket his copies of the contract and hoped that this friendly nonsense could soon be over so she could start working with the orchestra.

But evidently Mr. Margan thought she needed to be buttered up for awhile. He took her around to meet all the larger cogs in the organization and then treated her to lunch, which was the best part of it all. As Sarine cut her steak, she realized what Jerry had meant about being grateful to New York. The music business, as Sarine knew it, was the place where whoring and pimping flourished most luxuriantly. Most of the top entertainers she'd met had gotten in on their tails; this was accepted practice which nobody thought about twice. Yet, because of Jerry, she had never found it necessary to indulge in that kind of sexual barter.

She watched Jerry finish a highball and hoped that he could make it through the afternoon without getting sick. In a strange way she loved this man and wished that she could do more than just earn money for him.

After lunch Mr. Margan took her over to the studio and Sarine went gladly to work. Thanks to a good arranger, the orchestra captured the feel of Paul's music and Sarine gave herself to it with every nerve of her being. She yielded to the melody as she had never yielded to Paul.

Day after day, she forced herself to higher efforts, not permitting herself to be satisfied if so much as one bar did not ring with the peak of her feeling.

When Sarine finished the album, she secluded herself in her hotel room for a week and let her tense nerves begin the slow process of unwinding. She cried without feeling sad. The tears sank into her pillow and she sobbed herself to sleep every night. Perhaps it was the natural result of supreme effort. She did not question her emotions or try to explain to herself.

No one bothered her. Jerry called once or twice a day to check up on her. She knew he understood without either of them having to mention it. She knew, also, that he turned down offers for her to work.

When she came back out into civilization, Sarine saw her album in the windows of department stores. When she turned on the radio, she heard herself singing. Juke boxes in bars and luncheonettes carried selections of her music. Kids stopped her in the streets for autographs.

No matter how much money she spent, her bank account fattened on the royalties which poured in. She moved to a penthouse apartment overlooking Central Park. High above the ground she was insulated from the city's pulse. In privacy she could sit at the piano and pick out parts of other songs she had not recorded. Jerry bought her diamond earrings larger than the garish rhinestones she'd worn during the early part of her career. Everyone knew Sarine Duvalle. And Sarine Duvalle knew everyone.

But the only place where Sarine could really feel at all content was Jerry's flat in the Village. Often she would make him take her there in the evening. The place had no telephone. They could relax for as long as they wished.

One night, as they were sitting on the couch eating sandwiches of Italian ham, Jerry said, "Maybe you'd like me to get you a place like this so you won't be jealous."

She smiled at him around the roll and took a swig from the soda that stood on the bare wooden floor.

"Maybe," she said. "But not just now. I like the excuse of being here with you. I don't think I care to be alone. Not even far from the maddening crowd."

"Okay," he said. "You'll let me know when."

Sarine nodded. "But you can make another key for me, if you'd like."

"Sure."

They finished their sandwiches and played a quiet game of checkers. Each concentrated on the moves as though the game had some special importance. Sarine glanced at Jerry now and then to find him deeply engrossed, his eyebrows brought together to form a deep vertical wrinkle in his forehead.

After she had won the game, Jerry said, "I've got a bit of news for you."

She saw that he was trying to act casual, but he must have been wrestling with whatever he had to say. Jerry had never played checkers so slowly. Nor did he often lose to her.

"Go ahead," she said, just as casually yet absorbing his odd disturbance.

Jerry gathered the red pieces and set them into place. "We located your boy," he said. "Or rather, he got in touch with us."

Sarine felt her heart begin to clench and unclench like a fist within her.

"Who?" she asked, not daring to assume any meaning behind Jerry's words.

"You know who." Jerry glanced sharply up at her. "Forde's the name, isn't it?"

Sarine was speechless. Her eyes beseeched Jerry to go on.

"I got a letter this morning." He reached over and pressed Sarine's hand gently. "Nothing much. Just a brief note to say he'd be in town to settle about the money we're holding for him. And he did send you his regards."

Sarine tried to shrug it off but her lips were dry and the smile felt clumsy on her face. "Good," she said in a brittle voice. "I'm glad he's showing a little sense at last."

She forced her fingers to move the checkers around the board.

Jerry, in all kindness, let her finish the game without forcing further conversation. There were so many questions rattling around inside her, but she knew Jerry anticipated them and would have answered them without her having to ask, if he could.

They played half a dozen more games until Sarine got control of herself. Most of all, she realized that Paul didn't particularly wish to see her, now that he had finally broken his long silence. Did he hate her? Was he not able to forget that night they'd spent together? Perhaps he thought that Sarine despised him. But if he'd received her letter, he must know that was not the truth.

The thought of Paul's sudden closeness after all this time was frightening. How should she behave when they finally met again?

If they met. Sarine did not fool herself into assuming that Paul would naturally seek her out just because he was coming to New York. It would be just like him to take his money and leave without any meeting between them. Perhaps it would be better that way.

"Maybe you want to spend the night here?" Jerry offered.

She smiled at him gratefully. How perfectly aware he was that she didn't want to be left alone. Stalking from room to room, a victim of her own emotions, was something that Sarine must avoid for tonight. Of all things, her pride was causing the discomfort. She had assumed Paul's friendship only to discover that this friendship was not returned. She had lent a helping hand to Paul and found it rejected. Sarine suddenly wished violently that

Paul had never come into her life. They weren't the same kind of people and they rubbed against each other harshly.

Jerry took her out for a beer, then walked with her for many blocks so she could get some of the tension out of her system.

When they returned to the apartment, she took Jerry in her arms and tried desperately not to think of anything more important than the fleeting kisses they shared.

Thank heaven, Jerry's body still made her own pulsate in response. She had learned the habits of his love-making and found them congenial. The little room with two narrow windows overlooking a crooked street made Sarine feel very safe from the necessity to resolve the problem of Paul. In this apartment, she was just an ordinary woman making love with an ordinary guy. And Paul could not intrude upon this.

The beer on Jerry's breath did not repel her. She felt glad that he was human with faults and vices that Paul would never share or understand. Perhaps that was Paul's trouble. His inhuman strength of character would require a woman with no personality of her own.

"Dear Jerry," she whispered and slid her hands inside his shirt to feel the beating mortal heart which was so much like her own.

They lay on the couch, kissing each other unhurriedly. Jerry's eyelids were closed and his hands moved along her body with the knowledge gained from many nights of such pleasure.

Sarine liked the way he manipulated her flesh. Jerry knew how to make all parts of her come alive beneath his touch. He seemed to switch parts of her on as though her body were composed of a string of electric lamps. With no other man had she enjoyed such mutual passion. In a way she felt she belonged to Jerry because he had pioneered the way to her desire. If only they could love each other as others loved.

The chill night air swept over their bodies and Jerry eased himself away to light pieces of wood in the fireplace. They sat in the orange glow and listened to the windows rattling loose in their frames. Outside a young boy called to his friend down the street. His voice, high and urgent, filled the serenity of the warm apartment with alien needs. Sarine wished they could be on a mountain top where no one and nothing could touch them.

But Jerry, with his particular wisdom, left Sarine's body unsated. Goaded by desire, she could not think too intensely about Paul. Her mind focused on the animal drive which placed pleasure just out of reach. The intense urge toward fulfillment blinded her to everything else. And Jerry did not yield until the logs had burned out, leaving a shudder of blinking, dying cinders.

When Sarine came back to her own apartment, she felt a strong desire to be with people. The worst thing that could happen to her would be to remain alone for too long a time.

She picked up the phone and called Sam. Even an old man was better company than none. And Sam took her to all the better restaurants. He enjoyed being seen with a young girl. Perhaps it implied a physical prowess of which he had long since been incapable. At any rate Sam was pleasant enough company.

But even after a night with him, Sarine still had to come home to herself. She felt as though her apartment were a huge waiting room and no sooner had she closed the door behind her than she wanted to run out again. Life was becoming one long vigil as Sarine waited to see if one day she might accidentally run into Paul somewhere.

Sarine made the mistake of telling herself that her state of nerves resulted from overwork. She began sleeping at other people's apartments, not caring who they were.

Sam accepted her company with delight. His wife dead these many years, his children married and busy with their own concerns, Sam was free to cater to himself as he wished. And he took on Sarine as his personal hobby.

She camped at his home in Long Island for weekends at a time. He showed her photographs of his grandchildren and chortled toothlessly over bright sayings that had been conveyed to him by one of his daughters-in-law.

"And you too," he told Sarine. "A fine girl like you should make lots of babies."

Sarine agreed with him, secure in the knowledge that he couldn't do anything to help her achieve this goal.

She played pool with him in the wood-paneled den and viewed films that he'd smuggled in from abroad years ago.

But Sam had other interests besides these vain longings for sex which had passed so far out of his reach. Sarine couldn't go on taking advantage of his hospitality without becoming a nuisance.

And so she left him and went back to the city. For awhile she preyed on Jerry who was very willing to spend with her whatever free time he had. The only trouble was that he didn't have enough of it. Often he would make engagements, only to break them at the last moment because a new client had arrived in town.

Sarine found herself face to face with her own disturbed image in the mirror. Her eyes were large and dark with dread. She had never known this feeling and it leaped within her uncontrolled and beyond reason.

She told herself she was being foolish. But the good sense made no impression. Her appetite, which had always guaranteed sumptuous curves, began to dimmish. And her cheeks grew paler though she spent hours fighting her way through windy streets.

If only Paul would come out of the darkness so she could see him and get it over with. Of course her imagination was making the situation more important than it had ever been. The mystery of Paul was what irked her, she told herself many times. If he behaved like a normal person, she wouldn't be consumed by this sense of drama.

In a final effort to dispel the eerie impatience which trailed her, she told Jerry to get her another engagement.

"About time," Jerry said.

In a week he had a spot for her at the Town House Roof. Once again Sarine bathed herself in the soothing music which alone could calm her. Purposely she sang only old tunes and ballads because she was convinced that Paul's music had wound a spell around her and it was about time that she broke herself free. She would not sing any of his songs for awhile. But the audience clamored for encores from her album.

She couldn't get away from Paul's melodies. They were as much a part of her as her own voice. And so Sarine resigned herself to this and promptly forced herself to disconnect the melodies from the man. She almost achieved a respite from her unresolved anxiety.

And so Sarine did not know whether to thank Jerry for warning her or to curse him for goading her when he phoned one night to say that Paul was due at his office the following afternoon.

CHAPTER EIGHT

When Sarine put down the receiver, she saw that her fingers were trembling. She knew that even if she didn't go to Jerry's office tomorrow, she must inevitably run into Paul. Unless he made a determined and purposeful effort to avoid her, the music would bring them together. And Sarine, in spite of herself, was frightened.

The next afternoon she went to the movies at the hour of Paul's appointment. She did not want to be where Jerry could reach her. And safely hidden in the theater, she would not have to fight her own impulses which perversely drove her to confront Paul.

Later that evening, when she knew it was safe, Sarine telephoned Jerry. She accepted a dinner engagement with him though her appetite was completely shredded by nervousness.

Jerry met her outside a small Italian restaurant down in the Village.

"You're blue with cold," Jerry said. "How long have you been standing here?"

She didn't feel cold. She felt numb with whirling thoughts.

"It's my thin California blood," she said. Perhaps if she acted casual, she might begin to feel casual.

Jerry led her inside to a corner table and ordered two glasses of chianti. The warm aroma of garlic and cheese came from tables where others were applying themselves to the rich and spicy food. The undercurrent of chit-chat and laughter made Sarine's silence the more noticeable to Jerry.

"So." Jerry sipped at the red liquid and Sarine waited for him to finish considering how to impart his new knowledge to her.

"I have at least one word of encouragement for you," Jerry said. "Your boy is going to be in town for a couple of months."

"My boy?" Sarine responded with annoyance. "I wish you would stop assuming that I'm a lovesick pup." She took a long swallow of her chianti and found the taste bitter.

"Okay. Let's not argue. I'll give you the facts and you can do with them as you will."

"That's better."

A waiter offered Jerry a menu but he waved it away and ordered two antipastos.

"Mr. Forde has decided to take advantage of his musical talents and pursue his composing. Believe me, I didn't even have to talk him into it. He likes the green stuff as much as we do."

Sarine listened to Jerry speaking about Paul and it sounded as though he were talking about a stranger. Could Paul have changed so much now that he actually liked New York and wanted to live here? Every word Jerry said was in direct contradiction to the Paul she had once known. The idea of Paul being eager for money made Sarine unreasonably angry. What had changed him? Could this new success have spoiled him so quickly? She wouldn't believe it until she saw proof for herself.

"Did he—"

"No. He didn't ask for you." Jerry poured oil and vinegar over the salad and began to roll an anchovie around the prongs of his fork. "But he said to send you his regards."

"Well, when you see him again, you can send my regards back."

She could feel something different and very restless taking over inside her. Paul was here in the city. For ten cents she could hear his voice if she wanted to. He seemed to hover just beyond her reach, yet somehow very close.

"Tell me about his music." She wanted to hear Jerry talk about Paul. The words seemed to increase Paul's closeness. They made him touchable.

"He didn't bring anything with him. But he said he's got a couple of things in the trunk that should interest us."

"Us?"

"Yes, us," Jerry watched her pick up an olive and make a brave attempt to eat all of it. "You're not very hungry," he chided.

"Oh, shut up."

"Whoops. Little girl on a fast merry-go-round, now you listen for a minute. I'm not interested in your personal feelings just now. But I don't want them to get in the way of anybody's career, least of all your own. Paul didn't say he wished to avoid you or stick darts in your back. In fact, he was very civil and a pleasure to deal with. I must say, I didn't expect it of him. But people wise up when they get themselves a little cash and you ought to be glad that Paul is taking a nice, cool, businesslike attitude."

Sarine didn't try to defend herself. Irritated with her own ridiculous blunderings, she attempted to finish the antipasto as an act of contrition. She had no desire to ask help of Jerry. Her confusion must remain a personal problem. It behooved her to cope with her own emotions and bring them into abeyance. Regardless of what she felt or did not feel for Paul, she promised herself to maintain an outward calm. First of all, she would bridle this leaping curiosity. In time she would see Paul; then she would know, finally, what she must do and what she must feel.

She refused Jerry's offer to go to his hideaway apartment. It did not occur to Sarine that she wanted to be home in case Paul should have the sudden urge to call her.

Alone with herself, Sarine took a leisurely bath, reclining in the hot tub of water to smooth out and assort her thinking. Yes, it was all pride that consumed her. If she had been the one to leave Paul instead of him leaving her, she wouldn't be giving him a moment's thought now. Accustomed throughout her life to being the aggressor and the victor, she couldn't allow Paul to usurp her position. He had wiggled out of her confident grasp.

Facing this issue squarely put Sarine more at ease. She wrapped herself into a silk lounging robe, flicked on the radio and dialed a small Spanish station. Why should she entangle herself with Paul? What could he give her that she had not already attained for herself? This lovely apartment with its comfortable modern furnishings reflected her own tastes. She enjoyed contemplating the Matisse paintings on the wall; the blues and greens and reds vibrated in tune with her personal nervous system. And the Japanese floor mats felt good under her bare feet. How many years had she dreamed of buying all the things she wanted—these things?

And beneath this superficial display of her success ran a new vein of spoiled confidence. No longer did she need bravado to fuel her. Conviction and security had built strong foundations which she did not wish to give up.

Yes, Sarine had come a long way since the days of the Jingo Club. The subtle changes were very apparent even in the mirror. The wildness which had been her attraction no longer showed. She combed the black hair into a chignon, stately and sleek on her neck, and her make-up emphasized the upslanting eyes rather than the fullness of her lips.

Why should she endanger all this just to give herself the satisfaction of dominating Paul? She had been acting like a spoiled child, throwing a tantrum in order to get her own way. But Jerry had surprised her in the game. She was grateful to him for taking a firm hand with her. And, for everybody's benefit, she could subside into being a sensible lady. After all, she did not really believe that she loved Paul one iota.

And he could only get in her way. Unlike Jerry, he would not go along with her. Even if he had changed, Paul must still be very different from herself. Why should she make herself uncomfortable by trying to bend him to her own specifications?

Any personal involvement with Paul would make them both unhappy. It would be much better to deal with each other through the services of Jerry.

Satisfied with these conclusions, Sarine put herself to bed and slept peacefully through the night.

As the days passed and Sarine went dutifully about her business, the knowledge that Paul was in New York ceased to bother her. She accepted his presence as she had accepted it when they worked in the Jingo Club.

Ghostlike he presented himself to her through the sheets of music that Jerry presented to her for rehearsal. She looked at the pencilled notes and smiled in recognition of his familiar writing.

She took the music home with her and tried out the songs. The lyrics were less naive, perhaps a little brasher than the music she had known as his in the past. If Jerry had not convinced her that Paul was a changed man, the music did.

Sarine worked out her own style, then spent ten hours a day with the orchestra to make sure everyone did justice to Paul's new music. By the end of February, she was riding on a new crest of fame.

Her greatest satisfaction was the look of approval she met in Jerry's eyes. Four months now and neither had begun to tire of their relationship. In fact rumors were beginning to link their names with such epithets as "that fabulous duo."

Neither of them paid any attention to the catlike sounds hissing around their reputations. But any day Sarine expected Jerry's wife to extend her own claws in protest.

"Not Chris," Jerry said. "She's too pure to read gossip columns."

She had never heard bitterness in Jerry's voice before. It echoed dolefully through the Village apartment and Sarine hastened to change the topic.

"You know, Jerry, I think the time has come for both of us to take a vacation." The velvet slacks fit loosely about Sarine's waist and her entire body felt gaunt and tired.

Jerry refilled his glass with scotch. He didn't bother adding either water or ice, but drank the whiskey straight in one swift gulp without tasting it.

"Maybe so," he answered without enthusiasm.

"We could take a cruise to Bermuda or fly to Paris. How about that? Wouldn't you like a change?"

"Will you please stop acting as though you mean it?"

She took the bottle away from him and stood it on the windowsill. "But I do mean it. We're both overworked to death."

Just as she had put Paul out of her mind, Sarine also tried to ignore Jerry's drinking. They did both need a vacation; maybe if they got far enough away from New York, each of them could take a little breather and regain whatever it took to manage disturbing thoughts.

"Tell you what." Jerry poked at a log in the fire and tried to stir life into it. "We've got this big publicity campaign coming up for you. Right after you make those television appearances, we'll take off like a shot. Okay?"

That would be still another month, she thought. Anything could happen between now and then. She might even run into Paul.

"Okay," she sighed.

Once again Sarine entered the whirl of parties which attended each new onslaught of fame.

She received a printed invitation from Mr. Margan. On Friday next, he would be holding a gala affair at his estate in Connecticut. Automatically Sarine put the R.S.V.P. in the envelope and mailed it. She liked Mr. Margan because he didn't tell her how she should sing. He always approved of her recordings and bathed her in raucous laughter to convince her.

Partly because she liked Mr. Margan and partly because her afternoons were free, Sarine decided to have a special dress made for the occasion. She bought yards of ice blue silk and paid her dressmaker three times the usual price so that the gown would be ready in time.

All Friday afternoon Sarine went through a beauty ritual. She bathed and perfumed her body with different scents, each subtly blended into the other. Her skin, without its tan, had regained its natural marble whiteness. The pale complexion made her eyes larger and darker and perhaps a little older. She mascaraed the lashes into a heavy fanlike fringe, adding languor to the pattern of her features. The black hair she piled high on her head and wove through it a strand of tiny diamonds.

Complete, she viewed herself in the three-way mirror and decided objectively that the effect was magnificent. She recognized only the basic framework of herself, apparent in the ample hips and tiny waistline that emphasized her full breasts.

When Jerry came to call for her, his eyes traveled slowly over her body. "Chicken," he said, "you outdid yourself."

Sarine gave a soft laugh of pleasure. Compliments from anyone else were a dime a thousand, but a good word from Jerry was sparse indeed. He held her mink coat and she slid her arms along the white satin lining.

"Stand back," he said. "I want to get a complete picture."

Sarine obliged him. The silver blue fur draped in a luxuriant curve against the ice blue of her dress. Startling above this dazzling lightness shone the jet hair enhanced by the glittering diamonds.

"Oh, yes," Jerry murmured. "Yes, yes."

She swept past him into the hallway, almost embarrassed by his unaccustomed exuberance.

The doorman ushered them out and into Jerry's waiting automobile. As they drove crosstown and onto the Merritt Parkway, Jerry snapped on the radio.

"Turn the dial around," he said. "I want to hear you sing."

And Sarine played with the knob, her confidence just as sure as Jerry's that one station or another would be playing her records. Within five minutes a disc jockey announced one of Sarine's numbers. They sat back and listened to her voice fill the darkened car as Sarine watched the headlights carve out of the night yellow patches on the road.

"You've come a long way, little girl," Jerry murmured.

Sarine pulled the coat tighter around her shoulders. She gazed out to where bleak silhouettes of trees veined the moonlit sky. How cold and brittle the land seemed, out beyond this automobile.

"I love it, Jerry. I love having everything."

Within an hour and a half they reached the gravelled driveway of Mr. Margan's estate. Shining limousines stood parked in the garage area. Jerry pulled up beside them and escorted Sarine to the expanse of staircase which led upward past Doric columns to the wide brick door. Mr. Margan's house had started out to be of Georgian design, but his feeling of wealth had made him elaborate on the conservative lines. A butler opened the door and Sarine stepped inside where huge squares of black and white marble gave her the feeling of entering a Roman orgy.

Earlier arrivals stood sipping cocktails and exclaiming over each other's latest accomplishments. Still freshly groomed, still well-mannered, they moved gracefully into ever changing groups.

"Well, here come the twins." Mr. Margan thundered up to them and puffed a kiss against Sarine's cheek. "We've done it again, haven't we? The whole world is singing our songs."

Sarine gave him a friendly smile. "Thank you, Mr. Margan, for the opportunity."

Mr. Margan put a hand on Jerry's shoulder. "When are you going to tell her she can call me Bill?"

"Tell her yourself," Jerry said, reaching out to whisk a martini from a waiter's tray.

"How about that, Sarine?" Mr. Margan shifted his hand from Jerry's shoulder to hers.

But a silly quirk prevented her from calling this man Bill. He seemed too huge for the single syllable.

"All right," she said. "I'll practice."

She let Mr. Margan take her further inside beyond the staircase where two oak doors opened to the living room. Blondes and brunettes chatted quietly with the men they would be in bed with later on that night. Overtly they flirted while their husbands spoke of business matters among themselves. A young boy with shining red hair newly tinted doodled at the piano. For a moment Sarine wondered to whom he belonged. Then, as he smiled at her, she realized he was just an escort-at-large.

"Darling, darling Sarine Duvalle!" A tall and almost chestless blonde came clucking across the room, both arms outstretched. "Your new album is just—"

But Sarine didn't hear the rest of the sentence. Her body went suddenly cold and her ears began to ring in a high eerie pitch.

Beyond the woman's shoulder, she had seen Paul, leaning against the side of a wing chair. And he was looking right back at her as though there were no distance between them.

Paul didn't take one step to come toward her. He tilted his head in an almost imperceptible sign of greeting. The nod gave Sarine a small bit of encouragement. This was his familiar subtlety, his habit of underplay, strong and steadfast as the hidden roots of a giant redwood.

Sarine nodded in return as the woman clung to her hand and jabbered on. Her blurred monologue gave Sarine a chance to calculate all the things that were different about Paul. The appearance which had once been soft, almost shadowlike, had changed into an abrupt masculine austerity. The masses of brown hair were gone. He wore a close crop which showed the bones of his temples. And it made his face longer, more angular as though his features were hacked out by a woodsman's knife. He was just as thin, just as tall, just as stooping. Yet beneath this she sensed nothing of his old passive acquiescence. She felt a new and lordly quality that filled out his dinner jacket with a strength of spirit, if not the weight of heavy muscle.

"Hey, there, I thought you were lost." Jerry came over and rescued her from the blonde. He took Sarine's arm and squeezed it very hard. Grateful for the steadying pressure, she accepted the cocktail he thrust between her fingers.

"Steady there," he whispered. "Don't spill it."

She took a few quick sips and winked at him. "Okay," she said. "Let's get it over with."

Jerry led her across the room, stopping on the way to greet Mrs. Margan and Sam, who was modelling a toupee. Inevitably they reached Paul.

"Hi," Jerry said. "Brought you an old friend. Recognize her?"

Sarine looked upward into the depth of green eyes that seemed to flicker like a keen edge revolving in light.

"No, I didn't recognize you at all, Sarine. New York has made you much too beautiful."

She hated the formality and almost wished that Jerry hadn't brought her over. But Paul's soft voice played about her like his music.

"You're not very much the same either." Her own voice, low and controlled, did not give away the frustration that made her want to slap Paul and scream at him, "Why? Why?"

"Money maketh a new man," Jerry said. "How goes it, old man? Satisfied with the new contract and all that?"

"Quite satisfied, thanks."

Sarine steered her gaze carefully away from Paul and let it relax on Jerry. "New contract?" She took another very casual sip of her martini. "Something happening I didn't hear about?"

"Oh, lots of little surprises." Jerry took out a pack of cigarettes and offered one to Paul. "For you too, chicken. I didn't have time to tell you sooner."

He didn't have time? They had driven together an hour and a half with nothing to disturb them. She wondered what kind of game Jerry was playing now.

"Then tell me," she said, a jagged edge belying her blandness.

"Have a heart, Sarine. We didn't come here to talk shop."

"I'll tell you," Paul offered.

"Well, if you people insist on a business conversation, I'm going to find myself some more interesting people to play with."

And Sarine watched Jerry saunter off. She smiled inside herself, feeling a great warmth toward Jerry. He had managed to preserve for her a legitimate topic of conversation just in case they did run into Paul tonight.

"All right," she said, sitting herself in the wing chair. "What's in store for everybody?"

From his great height Paul blew a trail of smoke even higher toward the crystal chandelier.

"First of all, we're doing what they call a friendly get-together on television. You know, the old pals work together routine. Then, your smart friend managed to wangle us a special concert at Carnegie Hall. I play, you sing. A program of the old Forde-Duvalle melodies, you'd call it."

Sarine listened, nodding her head matter of factly. But her legs were shaking so that she was glad to be sitting down. Why had Jerry arranged it so that she would have to work so closely with Paul for a period of many months? This meant money, of course; coupling their live talents would make a super-star attraction. But Jerry didn't need the money and neither did she. Neither did Paul now. Yes, Jerry was money hungry. But was he such a worshipper of the green that he must disregard Sarine's feelings altogether? He knew she didn't want to be involved with Paul so intimately. Oh, it wouldn't make any difference to her in the long run, but at least he should have spared her feelings now. Jerry must be harder than she'd realized. A wave of disappointment trampled on her bond with him.

"Why, Paul, I think it will be wonderful for us to work together again. We had some fine times."

"Yes, we did.

His fingers curved over the arm of the wing chair and she saw the pattern of blood vessels on the back of his hand. Once this hand had touched her and she had shamed it with rejection. He couldn't have forgotten. Nor would he forget. Perhaps someday he would tell her his reasons for disappearing so suddenly. But she knew the reasons; no letter written in haste on a plane could alter or erase the smallest words of denial and refusal she had spoken to him.

"Are you enjoying New York?" she said, watching the room continue to fill up with the dozens of strange fish that comprised the aquarium of a night life which ordinary mortals peered into only when they had a spare moment.

"Of course I'm enjoying it now," he answered. "Occasionally I miss the warm sand and that horrible odor of sea weed. But I guess I can fly out if the urge gets too strong."

"You can fly anywhere." She set down the empty glass and wished for something else to do with her hands. Remembering her stage training, she placed one diagonally atop the other on her lap.

"All of us in this room can fly anywhere," he said lightly. "Isn't that a heck of a thing?" For the first time, he smiled the old Paul smile. The expression managed somehow to enhance the cleft in his chin.

"Tell me," she said. "Did Cozy really try to mash your brains in?"

He was about to answer when she saw his glance catch on somebody coming toward them through the doorway.

Sarine followed his glance to the pale redhead. No, it couldn't be true, she told herself. Silently, as if caught in a guilty act, neither she nor Paul attempted to renew the conversation as the woman came slowly and weakly toward them. The only bright things were the freckles on her face which seemed to stare through the translucent skin.

"Oh, Paul," she said, ignoring Sarine. "I'm sorry to be acting like such a baby, but those feathers in my stomach just won't go away. They have me exhausted."

"I'm terribly sorry," Paul said with sincerity. "Would you rather leave?"

"Oh, no. I wouldn't want to spoil all your fun. I'm such a nuisance as it is."

"Don't say that." He took the woman's small hand and held it hidden between his immense palms. "Darling, you remember Sarine Duvalle."

"Oh, yes, of course." She seemed now to collect herself and gave Sarine a bright superficial smile.

He turned to look down at Sarine, the formality completely formed again in his manner. "This is my wife," he said.

"Anna, naturally," Sarine said. "Won't you sit here and rest for awhile?" She rose before the woman could protest and watched Paul place her gently on the cushion.

Tiny, almost hidden in the mammoth chair, Anna looked up at Sarine like a little brown bird waiting for the chick to fly.

"You're such a marvelous success, Miss Duvalle. Paul and I are always talking about you." She reached up and pressed Paul's fingers.

"That's very kind. But it's Paul, of course, who deserves most of the credit."

What disaster, she wondered, could have befallen this poor man to make him want to marry such a jealous, clinging hypochondriac? She felt something deflate inside her. Perhaps her evaluation of Paul had been completely wrong. But she remembered clearly how Paul had treated Anna. Never had she seen signs that he cared for her. In fact, he hadn't even realized that Anna was chasing him. What profound despair had allowed him to be caught by her? Or maybe he had discovered a hidden feeling for this person who offered a secure promise of domesticity?

She searched Paul carefully for signs of love. He ministered to her every complaint with patient attention. Anna did not let go of his hand and he contented himself with awkwardly managing his cigarette with the other.

"If you'll excuse me," Sarine said, "some old friend just came in whom I must say hello to."

"Of course," Anna said in her pathetically cultivated little voice. "But hurry back to us."

"I'll try."

She nodded once again to Paul and drifted away.

If she had ever felt anything for him, if she had ever worried about feeling an adult emotion toward this man, the burden of her troubles now fell from her shoulders, leaving her light and free and ready to enjoy herself for the first time in ages.

Sam intercepted her.

"I like you bald," she said, taking off his toupee and folding it into his pocket. "This kind of thing is for old men. Not you." She kissed the top of his pate and kept on going past him until Jerry caught her and stopped the flight.

"Never fear," she said to his inquiring glance. "I couldn't feel better if I had just been born all over again."

"Good," he said. "That's my girl."

And to celebrate her release, Sarine consumed cocktail after cocktail, mixing them inside her without thought of the consequences. She wanted to get very drunk. Inebriated she could release the joy completely. No more Paul to worry her. The road ahead lay clear and swept clean of obstacles. Up, up, up the ladder she would go now. Her golden star would shine large and bright for all the years until her grave.

"Don't you think you've had enough?" Jerry said an hour later.

"Never enough," Sarine told him, freeing her wrist from his restraining hand. "I'm on my way to having a ball," she said.

Tonight she would fling herself clear up to the heavens. Because tomorrow and tomorrow she would be working with Paul. Rehearsing lines with him, watching him roll up his sleeves and refrain from cursing when he got exasperated. Or did he curse now? Only Anna knew the answer to this question. And undoubtedly Anna would be right beside Paul every moment of Sarine's time with him.

Oh, she couldn't care less about this pathetic woman. But a tremendous loathing for Paul made her cringe all over. And no amount of whiskey could erase the taste of this loathing.

CHAPTER NINE

"JERRY, ARE YOU the world's number one bastard?"

"Certainly, chicken. I thought you knew that from the beginning."

Sarine noticed that the door stood ajar and Mrs. Reinhart's typing was slow enough so that she could listen. She went over and pushed the door shut with the side of her shoe.

"All right, laugh at me if you want to. But what you don't know is that I don't give one hoot in hell about working with him. I wouldn't care if I had to play a movie version of Romeo and Juliet with him. But what irritates me to death is that you permit that phony wife of his to hang around all the rehearsals. If you want that telly show to go smoothly, she's got to get off our backs. One more episode like yesterday's and I walk out. Believe me, Jerry, I'm not fooling."

Jerry found a paper clip and started to untwist the wire. Their two coffee cups stood half empty on the desk. Neither of them had felt much like eating lunch today.

"Fine," he said. "You're one hundred per cent right. But I'm not directing the show. She sits very quietly in her little chair and swallows her assortment of little pills every half hour. Can anyone accuse her of being a disturbance?"

Sarine's exasperation throbbed in her throat. All week long she had tolerated the triumphant smirk that gave Anna's face its pale light of satisfaction. For the first two days Sarine had ignored the woman. And if she had kept her mouth shut, Sarine would have continued to ignore her. But after each rehearsal

Anna always managed to niggle her with some sweet little dig, and Sarine was finding it difficult not to squash her with a few choice words of her own. But for Paul's sake, she didn't want to cause dissension. She didn't want to embarrass him by emphasizing the pettiness of this creature he had chosen to make his wife.

Jerry said, "I'll make a deal with you. Try it just once more this afternoon. If she pulls anything, I'll speak to Abram. He's the only one who can bar her from rehearsals."

"She will, all right."

"Fine. Then you'll win your point."

She didn't want to win any points. All she desired was a little freedom to do her best for the show. Appealing to Jerry was the only way to accomplish this with decency. In the old days, she wouldn't have thought twice about turning a woman like Anna upside down with words that could make a merchant marine dizzy. Yet something restrained her, and at rehearsals she maintained a ladylike pose. But her patience to continue this act was ebbing fast.

Sarine picked up her stole and draped it over her arm while Jerry buttoned into his coat.

"Just today. Now remember," she said.

They rode down in the elevator and Sarine was so preoccupied with her aggravation that she hardly paid attention to Jerry's casual banter.

Because they arrived at the studio fifteen minutes early, Sarine went to the ladies' room to rearrange her windswept hair. Glad for this excuse to get away from Jerry's nonchalance, she took out an emery board and filed furiously at each of her ten long nails. She knew Jerry wasn't a man to lack insight. Especially when it came to herself, he was cued in on all the right channels. Then what, she wondered, were his motives for permitting Anna to pick on her?

If the woman weren't Paul's wife, Sarine could easily take care of the situation by herself. But under the circumstances it would be awkward, to say the least. She could so easily be accused of jealousy. And wouldn't that make juicy reading in the gossip columns? Even as she thought this, Sarine realized how odd it was that she suddenly cared about public opinion.

When she came back into the studio, she saw Paul straddling a chair on the stage. He held the script propped on the chair frame and appeared to be studying his lines. Anna, sitting in the front row of the orchestra, gave a little cough to announce her presence.

"Hi," Sarine said to everyone and took her own script from the large patent leather purse.

"Everyone's early today except Abram," Paul said. "He must be fed up with hearing the same thing over and over."

Jerry, seated two seats away from Anna, was pulling up the wick of his lighter. He didn't seem inclined to make amiable conversation but Sarine knew he was observing the interplay without appearing to do so. She felt like a specimen on a glass slide.

At last the back door opened and Abram came striding down the center aisle.

"Okay, folks, let's go," he said.

All during rehearsal Sarine tried to be as distant and cool to Paul as was humanly possible. Likewise, he paid very little attention to her, smiling only when the script called for a smile or squeezing her wrist affectionately when the stage directions ordered him to do this. Every day, at precisely ten past three, Paul had to touch her wrist. His dry palm touched her skin for a fleeting second, then withdrew again like the action of a puppet. Nothing happened and nothing was implied to arouse Anna's gall. No two people ever behaved more like unfeeling robots than Paul and herself during this supposed exchange of shared friendliness.

So Jerry should be satisfied that Sarine did absolutely nothing to provoke Anna.

Even Abram, as though to prove the point, said, "Can't you two kids warm it up a little? The folks watching you want glamour, sophistication, dreams." Artistically he tugged at his pointed red beard. "For Pete's sake, give it to 'em."

Paul wiped his forehead with a handkerchief that only Anna could have ironed so perfectly. "It's fine the way we're doing it," he said. To Sarine's observation, his cheeks looked more than usually gaunt. She wondered if Anna laced it into him every day when they got home.

"We'll do it again," Abram said in a voice that brooked no argument.

A tired sigh escaped just loud enough from Anna for everyone to be aware of her without actually being disturbed by the sound.

Without hesitation, Sarine started her lines over again. Perhaps if there were an emcee between them, the situation could appear more relaxed. But Abram thought that a moderator would break the air of intimacy so necessary for the act.

They went through their lines with the physical touches and sentences designed to simulate a feeling of nostalgia.

After the fourth time through, Abram said, "Okay, cut it. Tomorrow we'll pick up on the music bits. There'll be a piano on this damned stage, I hope."

As Sarine came down the steps, Anna said to her, "It'll be all right, dear, if you want to smile at my husband a little more often. You'll look more natural that way." She pressed the gold catch of her pill box and extracted a green tablet.

Sarine glanced at Jerry and he nodded almost imperceptibly.

As Abram pushed down the sleeves of his polo shirt, preparatory to leaving, Jerry said, "Let me give you a lift to wherever you're going. I'd like a couple of words with you."

"Sure, kid," Abram said. "But snap it up. I've got a million things on my back."

Jerry took Sarine's elbow and the three of them left Paul to help his wife into her sweaters and coat.

"Where to?" Jerry said, easing the car into traffic.

"The Ninety-Second Street Y. Now, what's on your mind?"

Sarine was sitting in the back of the car trying to make herself unobtrusive.

"I'd like you to do me a personal favor," Jerry said. "My property in the back seat has been as cooperative as you could want, hasn't she?"

"Sure. She's a sweet kid." He took out a pouch of tobacco and began rolling a thin cigarette.

"You appreciate that sweetness, don't you? The lack of a star's temperament, etcetera?"

"Always."

"Then how about helping us out by telling Paul to leave his wife at home from now on?"

Abram turned full around and grinned at Sarine. "You don't say so." The knowing look had a filthy twist to it. Sarine clenched her teeth so that she wouldn't blurt out the wrong words.

Convinced by her silence that his suspicions were true, Abram became suddenly congenial. "Be glad to do you the service." His voice, sinuous as opium, made Sarine's cheeks burn. "I'll call the boy tonight and give him orders." He struck a wooden match and applied the flame without taking his gaze away from Sarine. "Anything the lady wishes."

She could hardly wait until Jerry dumped him out at his destination.

"Well, now," Jerry said after Sarine had rearranged herself in the front seat. "That wasn't so difficult."

Sarine nodded. But she had the sickening feeling that this request of Abram had been one of her first major blunders.

She asked Jerry to drop her off at the Health Roof swimming pool.

"Want company?" he asked as she started to get out of the car.

Sarine shook her head no and he drove away without asking for an explanation.

She went upstairs and got a towel and bathing suit from the attendant. Pushing her hair into the tight bathing cap and pulling the lastex down to blot out all sounds, Sarine began to feel a little bit further away from the sticky situation with Paul. The cold green water enveloped her body and she swam close to the bottom, her hands now and then touching the slippery tile. This shimmering world of blurred arms and legs above her gave Sarine a moment's respite. She felt unreal and safely far away from her usual reality. No need to think here in this water. Her body stretched and coiled and stretched again in a slow breast stroke, giving physical release to her emotions.

When she came up for a breath of air, her intuition of disaster had dissipated itself enough for her to be comfortable again. She had no actual reason not to trust Abram. He had nothing to gain by making her relationship with Anna tenser than it already was. Even if he had a strain of nastiness that would enjoy watching a cat fight, he had enough sense not to let it get in the way of his show.

For two hours Sarine worked out in the pool. Nobody bothered her or tried to make conversation. The few pairs of eyes that found and dwelt on her curves beneath the wool suit remained sufficiently unobtrusive. From the activity of swimming her blood began to circulate through the tired limbs. A surge of renewed briskness lifted her attitude to more optimistic levels. The burden of Anna slid away from her along with the drops of water.

Sarine took herself to supper, then went home and enjoyed a dreamless sleep.

The next afternoon, Jerry's schedule of appointments prevented him from accompanying Sarine to rehearsal. She didn't mind. She didn't even care very much. Her self-confidence was enough of an escort now.

Sarine arrived at the building a few minutes early and met Paul there waiting for the elevator. She noted with gratification that he was standing alone.

"Hello," she said pleasantly and made no mention of Anna's obvious absence.

"Hi." He put the butt of his cigarette into a sand-filled urn. His features, perfectly composed, gave no indication of what had transpired with Abram.

They stood awkwardly without speaking further. She wished she could discover whether Paul was glad or not that Anna could no longer accompany him. She thought he was glad for these few hours away from her thousand little hooks.

"Nice day for walking," she said. "The wind pushed me all the way across Fifty-Seventh Street."

She stepped into the elevator and watched Paul take off his gloves. They were heavy wool knit, and Sarine instantly knew that Paul wore the ugly things because Anna had made them. He stuffed one into each pocket of his raincoat. Paul wasn't the kind for bulky clothing. His lean body could go through spring, fall and winter dressed in the same corduroy jacket.

Paul held the studio door open for her and as she passed by him he whispered, "Let's give Abram a bang-up job. Maybe we can get out early for a change."

She nodded, wondering behind her smile whether Paul was anxious to get home to Anna or whether he would ask her to go for a stroll with him.

"Okay," Abram said, "let's have a quick run-through and got to the piano they finally decided to give us." His eyes slitted with tacit acknowledgement of thanks from Sarine for the favor he had done her.

Sarine went on stage with Paul and each took a chair. Paul sat with his legs outstretched instead of politely crossed.

"It looks better already," Abram said.

Sarine began her lines and Paul blended in with an easy flow of dialogue. Their words sounded spontaneous now instead of memorized. And when Paul squeezed her wrist, he gave her a wink and a smile that Abram applauded.

Then Paul went to the piano and played casual snatches of melody. Sarine warmed, hearing the old style, the familiar touch. When she sang, her voice had an extra quality of richness missing before. Complete in her satisfaction, Sarine sang with recaptured joy.

"Remember this one?" Paul said, responding with his own pleasure.

Before Abram could stop them, they were launched into a journey of music that recaptured the old days, the devilment, the beat, the lack of responsibility to anything but music.

"Have it your own way," Abram said when he finally managed to call a halt. "But don't you dare get out of hand like this Sunday night."

Like two delinquent children, Paul and Sarine agreed. Then immediately they returned to the songs as Abram put on his cap and left for the day.

Sarine, unbridled by a sense of time, followed Paul from one lyric to another. She watched his face calm with inner enjoyment. Lost in the music, he played countless variations of the old tunes. They laughed and recalled episodes at the Jingo Club which hadn't seemed very funny at the time.

A handyman came in, announcing his presence with a discordant jangling of keys.

"If you folks're ready to leave . . ."

"My gosh," Paul said. "It's almost seven-thirty."

"So it is," Sarine said mildly. "And I'm starving."

For an instant they looked at each other intently.

"Is there a phone around here?" Paul said.

"Down in the lobby," the handyman replied.

As Paul helped her into her coat, he murmured, "The poor girl must be out of her mind by now."

She saw his preoccupation and made no further comment until after he came out of the phone booth. The pleasure now was washed completely off his face.

"She's in bed. What kind of a fool am I?"

"But she knows you're all right," Sarine offered, knowing her words were no comfort.

"Sure, I'm all right," he said irritably. "But she isn't." He hurried her out into the street. "Poor kid's hardly had a well day now that she's going to have a child."

Sarine became suddenly alert. Anna was pregnant? She could hardly believe that fragile body could carry another living being. All her irritation with the woman drained out and she felt within her heart a rumbling of shame. Sarine had never been one to take advantage of those who could not defend themselves. Her ruthlessness was a direct result of having to establish her own career. But now Sarine had everything and nobody could get in her way. To trample on someone like Anna made Sarine feel very small.

"I'm terribly sorry," she murmured. "Why don't you grab a taxi?"

They stood in the electric daylight of the avenue. The bitter wind flapped Paul's coat open but he didn't notice.

"Yeah," he said slowly. "I guess I'd better."

She watched him make his way through the traffic and climb into a cab almost before it had a chance to stop.

Deflated with self-disgust, Sarine wandered along the street. She couldn't bring herself to like Anna just because the woman was ill. But neither could she forgive herself.

The next day at rehearsal Sarine's first words to Paul concerned his wife.

"She's okay, I guess."

They went through the script and the music, doing things just the way Abram wanted so that he wouldn't raise his voice and distract them from their own thoughts. He let them off early and Paul convinced Sarine that it would be all right for him to have a cup of coffee with her.

"You're sure, now." She wasn't going to be the cause of any further trouble. It was one thing for Anna to be a hypochondriac but quite another if she had a threatening miscarriage.

"Yes, I'm quite sure," Paul said.

They went into a pleasant restaurant beside Central Park. The place smelled of sweets and the mirrored walls reflected the profiles of ladies taking afternoon tea with their pastries.

Sarine wanted to hear more about Paul's relationship with Anna but she hesitated to bring up the subject. It wasn't her business, after all, to discover the facets of Paul's private life. And yet Sarine felt a strong desire to absolve herself in some way.

On the other hand Paul wanted to talk about music. He hung up their coats and leaned forward across the table.

"I'd like you to try out a couple of new things with me," he said. From his back pocket he took out sheets of music paper and handed them to Sarine.

"They look good," she said. "May I take them home and try them out tonight?"

"But the chords aren't written down."

"That's okay," she smiled. "I can't play chords anyhow."

"Then you'll never get the feel of them." He looked at her with a disappointment which made his face very young.

"Well, what do you suggest?"

"Maybe we can go back to the studio for an hour."

Sarine shook her head with conviction. "No. First of all the place is locked up by now. And secondly, you're supposed to be home soon."

"I know, I know." He rapped the table impatiently. The sound of his knuckles seemed to accompany the rapidly moving thoughts.

"I'll phone Anna now. If she knows in advance that I'll be home late, then she won't worry." His green eyes looked at her hopefully.

"She might not worry," Sarine offered. "But she will mind."

"How can she mind if she knows what I'm doing?"

Paul's exasperation betrayed what Sarine had suspected all along. She could envision his life: boring, perfect domestic routine. Paul had been mistaken. He didn't really want the picket fence and roses. How much he hated it showed in the way he would not allow Sarine to convince him that he should go home. His lips formed a thin line of conviction. He'd made up his mind to stay out for awhile. Sarine couldn't change it.

He got up, dug some change out of his pocket and went to the telephone.

Waiting for him, Sarine sipped slowly at her coffee. She felt sorry for Anna and her futile struggles to make Paul happy. How he must have talked to her about the perfect marriage. Orange juice and scrambled eggs for breakfast. Idyllic love supreme. But what Paul thought he wanted and what he actually needed were two different things. How long, Sarine wondered, after his marriage with Anna was consummated did he discover that?

Paul, the quiet one. Paul, the untemperamental musician. She should have had an inkling that Paul was lying to himself the night he'd beaten up Cozy.

But just as Paul had convinced Anna, so he had convinced Sarine. Now, in possession of all he had said he wanted, Paul must be struggling to understand why he was so unsatisfied. She knew that the futile perplexity dogged both Anna and Paul with relentless cruelty.

He returned to the table with a renewed smile.

"It's okay. I told you she'd understand." He slid into his seat and gulped his coffee with a new enthusiasm.

"Well, where do we go from here?" he grinned.

Sarine hesitated. Then she decided the hell with being worried about his home life. They wanted a piano. She had a piano.

"We can go to my place."

"Swell. Let's go."

They walked the few blocks to her apartment house, striding eagerly along without conversation.

She threw open the door and switched on the lights.

"Quite a classy place," Paul said. But he didn't bother to inspect the rooms or say anything really personal about her success. He tossed his coat on the divan and went directly to the piano.

Sarine dropped her own coat on the arm of a chair and in a few minutes both were once more engrossed with chords and melody.

Paul rolled up his sleeves after awhile and Sarine kicked off her shoes. She found him a pencil which he shoved behind his ear. The world seemed very far away.

"Try it like this," Paul said after substituting a new rhyme.

"I like it better the other way."

"Well, try it."

Sarine tried it. They argued. Then they compared the new words with the old, saying them without the melody.

"I still like it better the other way."

Paul erased the new words. "All right, damn it."

And so the hours went, happily spattered with tiffs and agreements and more tiffs.

Finally they were finished.

"These are the new songs for the concert," Paul said. "You do like them?"

"Don't be stupid."

He swung off the piano stool and picked up a stray apple from the fruit bowl that displayed out of season peaches and apricots.

"You know," he said, "I really enjoyed myself tonight. Thanks."

Sarine felt a flush of embarrassment. "Why thank me? It's all in the interest of more money and more fame."

He polished the apple slowly on the side of his trousers. "Oh, yes. I forgot."

They looked at each other and Sarine felt strangely as though they were back on the California sand. Foil tilted against foil, she wondered why they had to fence with each other.

Without thinking, she blurted, "Did you ever get that letter I wrote to you?"

He bit into the apple and she sensed that he wanted to avoid their past. But why avoid it? What did all that mean now that Paul was safely married and she was secure in her ambition?

"Yes," he said after awhile. "I got your letter." He made a movement to brush back his hair. "You understand that I sincerely believed nothing good could ever come out of prolonging the kind of relationship we had."

"And you were right," she said.

"We both knew without a doubt what we wanted." He smiled, mocking their convictions.

"You'd better go," she said. "It's rather late."

"Of course."

He picked up his coat and started for the door, the apple still in his hand.

"I'll take that," she said.

He dropped the core into her palm. "We've got us a good show. Jerry should be proud."

"So am I," Sarine said.

He left her standing alone, to gaze at the half-eaten apple. How easily Paul had cleared away her bad conscience about their past. She knew he did not bear a grudge. What had happened between them was over and finished. And Sarine was glad. Perhaps in time they could reestablish some kind of friendship. They worked so well together. If Anna could permit Paul time away from home, she would have a happier husband.

Sarine went back to the piano and hummed again one of his new melodies. As her fingers moved idly over the keys, the doorbell rang.

Jerry came in looking very pleased with himself. He wore an exaggerated swagger calculated to amuse Sarine.

"Haven't heard from you lately," he said. "Things getting on well with Mr. Music, I trust?"

"Splendid," Sarine said.

For once she wished to be alone with her thoughts. Not that she couldn't share them with Jerry. But right now, she wanted to examine the evening without interruption. Jerry had a way of showing her sides of herself that she did not care to see.

"Of course—splendid," Jerry said. "I saw him leave just as I was coming down the block."

"Did you bump into each other?"

Jerry picked up the apple which was sitting on the piano and looked at it quizzically. "No, I didn't say hello. Thought it would be the better part of discretion to let him go home uninterrupted."

She took the apple from his fingers and dropped it on a plate. "Now look here, you're not going to accuse me—"

"Who said a word?"

The blue of his eyes was very blue and very intent. For once Jerry was stark sober. She hadn't often seen him like this recently. It pleased her and yet she knew that he must be occupied with something terribly important if he chose not to drink.

"The fact is," Sarine said evenly, "I brought Paul home to go over some music for the concert. That should please you."

"It does. It does."

"But?"

"No but's. No criticisms. You're a big girl, I'm sure. So long as you don't play hookey, I don't care what else you do."

This was Jerry's usual method of expressing disapproval. He had nothing to disapprove of this time. Sarine felt impatient with his probing.

"Okay," she said. "I'll give you all the facts. Then you can give me your cold opinions and we can spend the rest of the evening separately minding our own business."

"Oh there, there. You're acting like a kid caught with her pants down."

"But Jerry, there's nothing. I swear it."

"So why the irritation with me?"

How could she explain it to him when she didn't even know herself?

"Let's drop it," he said. "I'll take you to the movies and we can sit together like two nice old friends."

Apparently for no reason it occured to Sarine that she hadn't kissed him for a long time. Perhaps the hint of loneliness in his voice reminded her. Since she wasn't feeling exactly lonely herself, her rapport with Jerry wasn't quite solid. In a way she felt like a traitor. Without another word, she came up to him and put both her hands on his cheeks.

"We don't have to go to the movies," she said and kissed him lightly on the lips. "Why don't we stay here and act like two nice old friends?"

He tried to hold her at arm's length but she forced her way toward him and pressed her body against his. She held him firmly to her, not wanting Jerry to look into her eyes. She did not know what they might reveal to him. But whatever it was, she wished to keep it unknown to him.

She ran her fingers up the nape of his neck and into his hair. "You're such a nice guy," she whispered. "Why don't we put out the lights?"

"Is that how it is?" he murmured.

She moved herself slowly against him. "That's how it is."

Taking his hands, she placed them on her hips. His touch, strong and certain of her body, made her feel like the old Sarine again. As her flesh began to tingle with desire, Paul floated away to a safe place out of her mind.

"You've got the concert all worked out?" The words brushed against her earlobe as his lips touched it.

"Almost."

His hands came slowly up to her shoulder blades and then reached higher to the zipper of her dress. "You're a good girl. Trained you right."

"We'll have a capacity house," she said, as he moved the dress down past her shoulders.

"Standing room only."

Slowly she opened his shirt.

"Can we leave the lights on?" he said. "I want to watch you."

She felt better now about Paul. "All right."

His touch traced paths of desire along her skin. Lying beside him on the couch, she felt herself mounting toward full need of him. The taste of his lips was good and pure without the alcohol. Perhaps Jerry was beginning to get hold of himself. She desperately hoped so.

Unconsciously her hand reached upward to flick out the lamp which was shedding its light directly on their bodies. Now in the semi-glow of the indirect lighting, she allowed him to take her, giving of herself with complete abandon to his masculinity.

Afterward they lay in a film of perspiration, staying very still as the dampness cooled on their skins.

"You know," Jerry said casually. "I really would hate to lose you."

"What brings up such a silly thought?"

He leaned over and kissed her on the cheeks. "Don't forget, chicken, we're the Siamese twins. And one always knows where the other is heading." Then he got up, took a shower and went to sleep in her bed.

CHAPTER TEN

Usually Sarine dissected Jerry's remarks until she was quite satisfied that she understood his meaning. But this night, she couldn't be bothered. Perhaps Jerry made more sense when he was drunk than when he was sober. She remembered when they had first met how terribly sober he had been. Something of the old Jerry had begun to return since the night they first saw Paul at Mr. Margan's party. Jerry was becoming gradually more sure of himself and less inclined to discuss with Sarine his personal affairs.

She decided this was a good thing. Knowing too much about Jerry made her feel in a way indebted to him. She no longer desired to confide her personal troubles. Perhaps she didn't really have any.

In the bedroom she listened to his light snore and got quietly in bed beside him. She would always love Jerry but he had begun to feel like her kid brother; she must admit to herself that the intensity of her feeling for him was beginning to diminish. She wondered if this were happening to him also. How nice it would be if they could both taper off simultaneously.

For the next few days she saw very little of him. Abram, Paul and herself worked overtime polishing off the show. She tried to send Paul home to his wife but often he detained her at the studio to work on the songs for the concert. She could not refuse him nor did she want to. This bond of music did something to both of them that Sarine could not describe. Nor did she think about it very much afterward. No wife, no matter how prudish, could find anything harmful in her relationship with Paul. As long as her conscience was clear, nothing else mattered.

The night of the performance, Anna brought herself down to the studio. Sarine observed her carefully, trying to decide whether or not Anna deserved as much attention as she felt she needed. If Sarine wanted to believe that the woman was a hypochondriac, she could find no justification for this accusation. Anna sat in the front row orchestra, her body sunken into itself like that of a little old man. She had tied her hair in a small knot on her head and even from the distance of the stage, Sarine could tell the weakness with which her hands moved as she reached up now and then to fix a slipping hairpin.

The show went smoothly. Apparently oblivious to his wife, Paul reacted warmly for the cameras. He said his lines with a perfect sense of intimacy. His glance rested warmly on Sarine and pauses of affection punctuated his words. He touched her wrist at the prescribed time. But he also touched her shoulder or patted her arm when he felt the desire to do so. And Sarine responded to his warmth. She could feel when a performance was going off with a special zip. She almost forgot the camera as they chatted easily about their past.

Then they went to the piano and did the songs, intermeshing their talents so that the audience applauded with spontaneous delight. After the show, she and Paul did an extra number because the audience demanded it of them.

Sarine was adjusting her stole when Anna made her way up to her.

"Did you have a good time?" Anna said. Her voice trembled and Sarine could not tell whether it was from anger or from her physical weakness. Dark smears beneath the girl's eyes made her seem older and wracked with a hidden misery.

Sarine wanted to be kind. "I hope you're feeling better," she said. "Paul told me—"

"Paul told you," she said bitterly. "I'm sure you gave Paul enough opportunity to tell you lots of things, Miss Duvalle!"

Before Sarine could answer, Jerry came up and put himself between the two women.

He paid Anna a gentle compliment which gave Paul time to come over and collect his wife.

"Darling," Paul said. "You shouldn't have come up here."

"Why not?"

"The steps."

"You know I'd climb a thousand steps to see you."

Jerry led Sarine quickly away. "Supposing we duck out for a fast drive around the park."

She didn't particularly feel like going, but he had her by the elbow and was steering her out the door. Yes, the old Jerry was back in order, she decided. And she felt better. He could take care of himself. That's what made Jerry Lutha great. Not the drive alone, not the speedy intuition that could find and develop talent almost over night—but his uncanny ability not to go to pieces within himself. She felt wonderful for him and was happy to go for a drive through the park.

Hardly a week after the television show, Sarine began rehearsals with Paul for the concert. They had a room complete with piano and recorder. Nobody bothered them. The performance would be all their own without the need for useless words.

Paul would meet her at half past eight in the morning and together they went to the studio where they stayed until six. A boy brought lunch in to them. They had three weeks before the engagement. This comparatively short period of time was Jerry's personal tribute to his faith in their abilities.

Neither Paul nor Sarine was aware of how hard they were working. All Sarine knew was that when she got home at night, she took a light supper and fell happily into bed. For the first time in she didn't know how long, she felt neither restless nor lonely. In her soul and in her body she was a complete person that needed no one else beside her music—and Paul.

Still, she wanted somehow to reassure Anna. But what words could she say without being accused? Maybe Anna had a right to be jealous. Sarine shared something with Anna's husband which seemed to bring them closer than a merely sexual relationship could.

She decided to invite Anna to her own home as a starter in breaking the ice between them. Somehow she must convince Anna that her husband's fidelity had not lessened.

"How about it, Paul? Will you come to dinner with your wife this Saturday?"

A line of annoyance curved around his mouth. Sarine had disrupted their rehearsal.

"I don't know. I'll ask her."

"Please don't forget."

And after rehearsal, Sarine reminded him again.

On the day after the next, Sarine received a formal note of acceptance from Mrs. Forde.

Sarine invited Jerry and hired a servant to take care of the details. She wanted to give all her time to pacifying Anna. The woman had to be convinced that Paul's music was the only bond between Sarine and himself.

When she told Jerry, he said, "You're out of your mind."

"But it's done," she said triumphantly.

"All right," he sighed. "I'll do what I can to help."

Impatiently Sarine waited for Saturday. She dressed with special care to be conservative, putting on a high-necked dress of black silk that revealed the loveliness of her shoulders and breasts by concealing them with simple grace.

Jerry arrived first with a bouquet of flowers in hand. "For your funeral," he said.

She laughed and arranged the roses in a silver vase. The savory odor of roast filled the apartment with a homelike atmosphere.

"No funerals, Jerry," she laughed. "Tonight we're all going to begin the birth of one big happy family."

"That's what I've always said—Sarine Duvalle alias Mother Earth."

She gave him a highball, which he tasted and put aside. For awhile they chatted about neutral topics. Then Anna and Paul came in.

Anna wore a dark green dress which would have complimented her red hair if her tresses were vibrant with life, but the strong color of her clothing only emphasized how faded and worn she looked.

"I'm so glad you could come," Sarine said, helping her off with her coat.

"Are you?" Anna replied. Her tone was cold and rude, and Sarine began to wonder why she had accepted the invitation.

Paul took one of Jerry's cigarettes and the two men launched into a financial discussion. Sarine listened with surprise to this facet of Paul. He showed an amazing astuteness for figures.

"You have a lovely home," Anna said. "I don't think I could live in so many rooms all by myself. Even with Paul, I prefer something cozier. I guess it's the small town in me."

Sarine offered Anna a glass of sherry and noticed that Paul watched every sip she took. In his wife's presence, Paul seemed a different person from the one she knew at rehearsals. His nerves were obviously wrought into a chain of knots. He watched every move that Anna made, however guarded, even though his conversation with Jerry had become intricate.

And Anna made sure he didn't overlook her for a second. "Paul, do you have my pills?"

"No darling. I think they're in your purse."

She opened her bag and found them. "Oh, yes. How forgetful of me."

Jerry guided the conversation to the impending concert.

"I hope you'll have a program for me soon," he said, nibbling a bit of caviar and cheese. "The printers are on my neck."

"Oh, don't pick on these poor darlings," Anna said. "They work so hard practicing every day, how can you expect them to remember little things like a program?"

Paul looked at Sarine with a silent apology for his wife.

"You'll have your program," Paul said. "First thing Monday evening."

Dinner went along clumsily despite everyone's efforts to please Anna. She refused to find anything pleasant except when she talked about the pies she baked for Paul or the new suit she had bought him or their plans to build a little cottage on Long Island.

By eleven o'clock she was apparently exhausted. Sarine got her things and Paul said goodbyes for them both.

"We'll be seeing each other soon, I hope," Anna said. "Before the christening of our child. Paul is hoping for a girl. Isn't that strange?"

Paul's face went absolutely white. His eyes dilated with anger and embarrassment.

"See you Monday," he said abruptly to Sarine. He nodded at Jerry and escorted his wife out.

"So there," Jerry said when the door had clicked shut. "What did you accomplish?"

Sarine drummed her nails on the tablecloth and glared at Jerry. "Don't think I'm going to give up this easily," she said, her voice low and filled with steel.

"But why?" Jerry insisted. "What's the purpose of all this? You're making a fool of yourself."

"Maybe I am making a fool of myself but there's something I'm going to prove to that woman."

"I know," Jerry said, emptying one ashtray into another. "You're going to show Anna Forde that the great Sarine Duvalle is not in love with her husband."

"Right."

"Fat chance."

"Why?"

Jerry got his coat from the closet and dropped it over his arm. "Think it over, chicken. You'll know why." He kissed her lightly on the forehead and went out.

Sarine sat in a corner while the maid straightened up the apartment. Jerry was so sure of himself, so sure. Well, this time he would discover he could be wrong.

She spent most of Sunday working out suitable and indirect ways of conquering Anna. Sarine didn't expect to win her over in a day or a week, but as time went by and Anna saw that only music existed between herself and Paul, she would have to change her mind. The woman would gain some security, and with security would come a little more warmth.

Monday morning Paul met her as usual. The March morning had almost a hint of spring in it. The night wind had lulled into a gentle breeze and white clouds promised a sunny day.

Paul, oblivious to all this, spoke of the program as they strolled.

Of course, they argued about the order of the songs. Sarine had come to enjoy Paul's arguments much more than the quiet man who had played for her in the shadows. Though she didn't realize it consciously, a new zest whipped along through her veins. A day with Paul made her feel more vigorous than a work-out in the swimming pool.

"I think we should open with *Angel Face*," Paul said.

"If we start with the most nostalgic tune, what'll we use for an encore that'll be just as effective?" she said.

All morning they juggled the order of the songs. Even after lunch they still hadn't come to a definite agreement.

"All right," Sarine said, "we'll do it your way."

Paul smiled at her with satisfaction. "That's better," he said. "If we always do things my way, we'll save a lot of time."

"Phooey."

They both laughed and moved directly into rehearsal. Six o'clock came and went, but so much remained to be done that neither of them noticed the passing of the hours.

The next day Paul did not seem quite so enthusiastic. He played almost listlessly.

"What's the matter?"

"Nothing," Paul insisted. But he kept looking at his watch and they left promptly on time.

Sarine learned to recognize and interpret signs of argument and tension between Paul and Anna. More often than not, Paul met her with an expression that did not conceal his increasing troubles with Anna. Indirectly, Sarine tried to draw him out on the subject. He was guilty of nothing and he had nothing to hide; but he refused to talk, as though Anna were a part of his life better left unmentioned.

Two days before the concert, Jerry phoned to say that the house had been sold out. Sarine was due for a triumph that would speed her into the galaxy of established stars. She went to the concert hall and gazed at the tremendous photographs of Paul and herself. Passersby stopped and stared at her, nudging each other openly.

Yes, she would really be in the holy circle of which she had dreamed all her life. This concert would clinch everything; afterward she could name her own ticket—engagements in Paris, Rome, all the centers of the world. And less than a year ago she was swinging her hips for a hundred dollars a week. Sarine gave herself a big hug.

She went home again because Paul had decided that they didn't need to rehearse any longer. This was true. But she knew he was saying it in obedience to the pestering of his wife.

Yet the next day, contrary to his words, Paul got in touch with her and requested one last run-through. She said yes, of course and met him at the studio. But they found the door locked.

"Damn it," Paul said. "I forgot. I told the guy we wouldn't be using it today."

"Well, come on back to my place," she said automatically.

And so they went to Sarine's apartment. Smoothly they ran through the songs until both were completely satisfied without question.

"Okay, kid," Paul smiled. "See you tomorrow night. Good luck."

They shook hands. From her window, Sarine watched him cross the street to get a cab. The slope of his posture and those long steps were vividly clear to her even at this distance.

She stayed in the apartment, dreaming not of tomorrow but of the homage which would come to her as a result of tomorrow. She felt confident and eager. Nothing could get in her way now. She held the world just where it belonged: in the smooth palm of her manicured hand.

The hours fled by in contentment. She slept, awoke, had a leisurely breakfast. The phone began to ring and she took the receiver off the hook. Why speak to anyone and destroy the world she was constructing in her dreams? Jerry would pick her up at seven and take her to the hall. Until then she wanted to be alone and undisturbed, allowing herself this little time to appreciate herself.

A strong spotlight of sun fell on the bed where she lay. Sarine closed her eyes, enjoying the languorous warmth on her body. When the area of sunlight crept off the bed, she got up, showered, had a light lunch. Tonight there would be a celebration in Paul's honor and her own. But she didn't care about the party. Her celebration would be on the stage, where she could look out at the thousands of people crowding in to see her.

The sun went behind a cloud, then dipped down beyond the wooden fence of houses. Time to get dressed and ready.

As she was combing her hair, the doorbell rang. She looked at her clock. Not even six yet. Surely Jerry must be overanxious if he had come for her this early.

She went to the door and found Anna standing there, her eyelids puffy, her lower lip jutting in a determined pout.

"Come on in," Sarine said. "Bring Paul with you?" She maintained a smile of friendly nonchalance.

Anna came inside. "No, I didn't bring Paul." Her head trembled slightly and her voice was a tone higher than usual. "And I didn't come here to wish you luck." She was breathing heavily as though she had been running.

"Please sit down," Sarine said. "You're overstraining yourself."

"A lot you care about me." She wore a light coat and neither gloves nor hat. Her windblown hair straggled about her shoulders and her lipstick, hurriedly applied, went beyond the lipline.

"You think you're going to take Paul right out from under my nose, don't you? Bringing him here. Doing heaven knows what and pretending to be working on a show. I've watched you for a long time. And I know you're nothing but a slut."

"Now just a—"

"You can't stop me." Her voice had risen to a shriek. "And you're not going to get Paul. Over my dead body you will!"

She lunged at Sarine, clawing her nails into Sarine's cheeks. Sarine tried to push her away, but Anna clung fiercely. Sarine felt the skin of her face tear in long burning streaks. Violently she thrust Anna from her and the woman stumbled to the floor. She rose, came toward Sarine again and tried to kick her. The blow glanced off her shin.

"I'll kill you!" Anna screamed. "Kill you!" All the fury of her little body came at Sarine once again, hitting with her fists, kicking, cursing hysterically.

In self defense, Sarine slapped her. Anna fell backward and crashed into the table. With a little cry, she crumpled to the floor. Her eyelids closed.

Sarine saw a stain of blood darken Anna's dress around the thighs.

Horrified, she picked up the phone and called for an ambulance. Then she ran to the kitchen and dumped ice cubes into a towel. Rushing back, she lifted the woman's skirt and applied the cold pack to the bleeding area. Somewhere, some time, Sarine had heard that this was emergency procedure for a miscarriage. But the blood continued to flow, staining the carpet, Sarine's hands, her own stockings.

If only the ambulance would hurry. She could die here of a hemorrhage. The moments went by, seeming like hours. Sarine began to perspire with worry.

At last, two white-clad men arrived. They hustled Anna onto a stretcher. She continued to bleed, as though every last drop of her life were flowing away.

"I'm coming along," Sarine said in a voice that shook.

"Okay, lady."

She rode down in the elevator. Her gaze didn't move once from the still, wan face.

Sitting beside Anna in the ambulance, she heard the siren wail as the car moved rapidly through the streets. They wove in and out of traffic.

Faster, Sarine thought frantically. Faster!

They arrived at the big tan hospital and impersonal, calm doctors took Anna out of Sarine's sight. She paced up and down, oblivious of her own appearance.

"Isn't there anything I can do?" she beseeched an interne.

"You can let me clean those wounds," he smiled.

"I'm all right."

"Just for the record." He sat her down and dabbed an orange fluid on her cheeks. The intense burning made her aware of herself again finally.

"Thank you," she said, trying to muster control and steadiness. She took out a mirror and saw that the scratches were really very superficial. With make-up properly applied, she would look fine on stage.

Another doctor came out. “She’ll need a transfusion. Are you related? Can you sign for it?”

“Yes,” Sarine said. “I can sign.”

With trembling hand, she filled in the papers.

The doctor looked at her signature and said, “Don’t you have a concert tonight?”

“I think so,” Sarine smiled weakly. “Do you have blood for her?”

“Of course. We’ll locate—”

“But there isn’t time,” she protested. “Will you try mine? It may be the same type.”

“But you’ll never make the theater.”

“Never mind that.”

“You’re all right, Miss Duvalle.”

Sarine went with him and rolled up her sleeve as the precious minutes fled.

“You’ll do,” the doctor said. “Common garden variety.”

How could he joke at a time like this? But of course, doctors saw death every day of their lives.

She went and lay down, watching as a nurse put the needle into her arm.

The dark life-giving droplets flowed into Anna’s veins, but she didn’t move.

Sarine looked at the doctor questioningly.

“A fifty-fifty chance. Of course, the baby is gone.”

He took Sarine’s hand with a professional manner of assurance. “There’s nothing more that anyone can do now. A matter of time and her own powers of recuperation.”

From his tone of voice, Sarine knew not to expect a cheerful ending to this episode.

She let the doctor lead her back outside into the corridor.

“I guess I’d better make a few phone calls,” she said. With a tired sigh she went to the booth.

Paul would be on his way to the theater by now. Perhaps Jerry had gone to her place and was waiting there to hear from her. In her haste she hadn't locked the door. Sarine dialed her number. Fortunately Jerry answered.

And he was down at the hospital in ten minutes.

Her face told him the complete story. When he reached her side, Sarine collapsed into his arms.

A nurse brought her a sedative but she refused to drink.

"I'm all right." She looked at Jerry. "How are we going to tell Paul?"

"The same way you told me."

"Do it easy," she said. "Please be kind." She waited by his side as Jerry phoned the theater.

"Look," he said after hanging up, "you don't have to go through all this all over again. Why don't you drink that sedative and let me take you home?"

"I don't want anything. How can you let Paul face this all by himself?"

"Sure, chicken. I understand." He sat her down on a bench and put her head on his shoulder. "You know, this is why I didn't want Paul around in the first place. His music was good even then. But a sixth sense told me something, so I listened."

She tried desperately to throttle the tears. But they welled up of their own volition and flowed fiercely down her cheeks, burning painfully over the scratches.

Paul came running in. Jerry took him aside and Sarine heard him repeating the story.

The doctor came out again. "There's no use staying here. I'll phone you when there's a change."

"But I'm her husband," Paul said with desperate futility.

"I'll call you," the doctor repeated.

The three of them returned to Sarine's apartment. By the time they reached the door of the hotel, the entrance was already mobbbed with reporters and photographers. Jerry hustled Sarine through as bulbs flashed mercilessly.

Upstairs the tumbled apartment repeated the tale of Anna's vain attempt on Sarine's life.

Paul could not look at her. He bent down and picked up the vase but did not seem to know what to do with it.

"Don't blame yourself," Jerry said.

"Why not? I didn't marry her for love. I married her for spite and she knew it. Only I didn't know myself until…" His voice trailed off helplessly.

"Why don't you go to bed," Jerry said to Sarine.

She didn't hear him. She was looking at Paul and something inside her turned over and over.

"Spite?" she repeated.

"Come on," Jerry coaxed. "You need some sleep."

He lifted her up and put her to bed. She lay in the dark, fully awake, staring at the ceiling and waiting for the phone to ring.

Midnight chimed on somebody's clock. Later, Sarine watched the sky become gradually lighter.

And as the dawn washed gray into the blackness the phone rang.

The morning papers had Sarine's picture all over the front page. Jerry tossed them on the couch, then went to the kitchen to make scrambled eggs. Paul, who was standing at the window in the living room, stood as though he would never move from the spot.

"Come on, old boy," Jerry said. "Have some coffee."

"Paul, we'll both have some," Sarine encouraged.

She went to where he stood and turned him to face her. "She could have played the game differently," she said. Jerry, working in the kitchen, could not hear them.

"But you don't understand everything," Paul said. His eyes seemed very deep in their sockets, as though hiding troves of terrible secrets.

"I don't have to understand," she said. "No matter what the beginning, the end was of her own choosing."

"Listen to me," his voice shook with pain. "Cozy threatened to come to New York and get even with you. Because Anna saw us together in my room, I could think of no other way to prevent her from goading him into it. So I married her."

A peculiar kind of relief flooded through Sarine. Immediately, she felt guilty.

"Are you going to let this hang over you for the rest of your life?" she said.

"I don't know. I just don't know."

Jerry brought in breakfast and between them they got Paul to eat some of the eggs and a scrap of toast.

"I'd better go home," Paul said. "And believe me, Sarine, I don't know how to—"

"You already have," she said softly.

Jerry saw him out.

Sarine lay on the couch, not waiting to think or feel. Listlessly she picked up one of the newspapers and let her eyes roam over the print.

"Don't bother," Jerry said. "You know what they'll do with a juicy morsel like this."

But Sarine became engrossed in the columns. As she read, something of hope stirred inside her. Not hope for herself, but for Paul.

"Listen," she said. She read to him the passages that could mean only one thing—the public was eager to know more, to see the fabulous scamp with their own eyes and listen to her sing Paul Forde's songs. The world thought they had been lovers. And now the world wanted to cheer them on. Or jeer. But she and Paul were more strongly in demand than ever before.

"So what are you going to do about it?" Jerry asked.

A renewed fire began to flame in her. What was she going to do? Why, she was going to pester Paul into working again. Music was his life, and he had to live—with or without the burden of Anna on his conscience.

She wanted to phone him right away, but sense told Sarine to wait. Wait a month, six months until the scars healed for him a little.

Try as she might, her impatience would not submit to this good sense. After a week had dragged by, she got dressed and went to Paul.

The apartment, which had once been so cheerful, looked semi-demolished. Paul had gotten rid of most of her belongings. But stray pieces of furniture seemed beyond his control.

"Let me help," she said quietly. "I want to."

"I thought you wouldn't want to look at me," he said.

"Give me a hand."

Together they got rid of the remaining pieces and Paul took a room at a hotel.

Sarine called him every day. Their short conversations grew longer. He took her for a walk through the park. They watched a new leaf struggle out of its bud and went every day to see how it was progressing.

The days lengthened. Their conversation veered slowly back to music. Sometimes, when they turned toward Sarine's apartment, she took his arm and listened to a new lyric that had come to him the night before.

She didn't argue with his rhymes. Not yet.

One afternoon, she said, "Why don't we try that one out on my piano?"

He looked at her sharply. She could see the struggle going on behind the furrows in his forehead.

"Come on," she said. "I'm too curious."

She took him upstairs and made him sit down at the piano. For a moment he stared at the keys. Sarine said nothing. She was not going to push him. She wanted the satisfaction of seeing Paul act with his own strength.

He lifted his hands and brought forth the first sweet chord.

Sarine listened, smiled and began to hum.

"Yes, I like it," she said. "Have you got the words written out for me?"

"Where's a pencil?"

She brought the pencil and paper, watching gratefully as he scribbled the lyric.

The months began to fly by. Song after song piled in odd sheets on her piano. Occasionally Paul spent the night, finding it senseless to go home after a hard day's workout.

They went shopping together, began once more to argue about rhyme. Paul's hair, fully grown in now, fell over his forehead and was ignored.

All this while, Jerry sat patiently around the edges of Sarine's life. The more she saw of Paul, the less time she had for Jerry. Once in awhile the three of them went out together.

It was Jerry who first broached the subject. "Look, kids," he said, relaxing on Sarine's couch. "I hate to be a party pooper but don't you two think you've been goofing off long enough?"

"Goofing off?" Paul protested. "What do you think all this is?" He pointed to the stack of music.

"Well, if you don't mind me being practical, what good does that stack of dirty paper do anybody? Nobody hears it."

Sarine looked sharply from Jerry to Paul.

"I see," Paul said. "Put up or shut up."

"That's it," Jerry answered.

"Well, what do you want? Another concert?"

"Good idea. Before the fickle public forgets both of you altogether."

"I'll think about it," Paul said.

Sarine didn't try to make Paul agree; she had no intention of forcing him to do anything. A new policy born of her new relationship with Paul guided her now. He would be the boss, in charge of all major decisions. She might protest about a lyric or a rhythm, but performances would be strictly up to him.

For the next week they continued to work over songs and Paul did not once mention their conversation with Jerry. Then, one night they were watching the lights go on all over the city.

"Well, what do you think?" Paul said, rolling down his shirt sleeves.

"What do I think about what?" She wanted Paul to say the words directly.

"Would you like to give it another try and see if you can make it to the theater on time?"

Sarine turned away so Paul would not see her close her eyes in grateful thanks. For the first time since Anna's tragedy, he was able to speak about it with good humor.

"Why not?" Her tone was low, so he would not hear the tremor in her voice. "Wouldn't it be greedy of us to keep all this wonderful stuff to ourselves?"

"Then call the great man and tell him," Paul said. "Maybe it'll make some hair grow out on his head."

She didn't have to be asked twice.

Jerry came right over with half a dozen cans of beer.

The three of them sat up half the night working out a schedule.

"You folks got me just in time," Jerry yawned at five in the morning. "I'm going up to Vermont tomorrow. There's a youngster singing in some two-bit club who promises some great things."

Sarine smiled to herself as she visualized Jerry saying this just one year ago about a youngster at the Jingo Club.

Now Sarine and Paul began to work with a purpose. One spurred the other on to almost inhuman effort. But the long hours did not make either of them tired. In fact, Sarine noticed that Paul's cheeks were beginning to fill out, and she saw the lines around her own mouth relax into an appearance of rejuvenation.

Paul practically lived with her now. He slept on the couch or in the bed. Neither one seemed to think twice about this. Sometimes she would awaken during the night and look at his naked shoulders outlined in the silver moonglow. And Sarine grew to expect Paul to spend the night. When he went home for a change of clothing, she felt strangely alone in the apartment.

But Sarine did not expect him to touch her. Nor did she want him to. Her new attitude toward Paul had taken on a strange twist. She could not think of him casually, in the way she had considered her relationship with Jerry Lutha. And so she slept beside Paul with a bridled desire content to wait for its proper resolution.

They went to see Jerry's new youngster, who was opening at the Mocha Club. The girl, a petite ash blonde, put her sultry songs across with unexpected gusto. Her ample bosom filled and overflowed the gold lamé dress. Afterward, Paul took Sarine to the party which Jerry was giving for his new protegé. Sarine watched him guide the child through all the proper paces.

"She'll do well," Paul commented to Sarine. "But I'm afraid the competition'll be too strong for her." They winked at each other and clinked champagne glasses.

They went home slightly giddy and full of secret confidences about their impending opening night.

For days the newspaper carried the story. Photographers snapped pictures of Sarine with Paul at the Casino, of Sarine with Paul stepping into the theater. They posed for these pictures gladly.

"The more publicity, the better I like it." Paul squeezed Sarine's hand.

Sarine had nothing more to worry about. Her Paul had come to himself completely.

Opening night, Paul bought Sarine a corsage for good luck and Jerry had to battle a path for them to the stage door.

Handsome, tall, standing a little straighter in his tuxedo, Paul led Sarine out on the stage.

The audience began to applaud. The sound rose and roared louder and louder. Sarine looked up to the balcony and saw people beginning to stand up. She raised her hands for silence, but the applause thundered down over her. For a full five minutes, she stood with Paul beside her, listening to the acclaim. Like a welcoming crest that would ride them back into the hearts of millions, the applause rolled from the audience to the two standing on stage.

Sarine swallowed hard as she looked out to the thousands of welcoming friends whom she had never known and would never know by name. She turned to Paul. He kissed her on the cheek and went to the piano.

At last the applause subsided.

"Ladies and gentlemen," Sarine said with all the brave strength that now filled her. "I should like to present to you the music of Mr. Paul Forde."

Paul bowed slightly and struck the first chord to the silenced hall.

With the sound of his music, Sarine knew that they would be together until death parted them. Paul's kiss still glowed on her cheek with its promise.

THE END

www.ingramcontent.com/pod-product-compliance
Lightning Source LLC
Chambersburg PA
CBHW031027260626
47153CB00017B/2740

* 9 7 8 1 9 5 4 8 4 0 2 7 0 *